The Devil's Water

Also by Richard Wirick

Many An Incense-Bearing Tree
(Essays)

One Hundred Siberian Postcards
(Memoir)

Kicking In
(Fiction)

The Devil's Water

Richard Wirick

Ekstasis Editions

Ekstasis Editions America

Copyright © 2013, 2018, 2019 Richard Wirick
Cover art: Claire Turcotte
Author photo: Heather Culp

New edition published in 2018, 2019 by:

Ekstasis Editions America
840 Apollo St., Suite 100
El Segundo, California 90245
USA

Canadian distribution by :

Ekstasis Editions Canada Ltd.
2808 Prior St.
Victoria, BC V8T 3Y3
Canada

Visit Ekstasis Editions online at www.ekstasiseditions.com to view our current catalog.

LIBRARY OF CONGRESS CATALOGING-IN-PUBLICATION DATA

CIP DATA may be obtained from the Library of Congress.

ISBN hardcover: 978-1-7324458-0-2
ISBN paperback: 978-1-7324458-1-9
ISBN eBook: 978-1-7324458-2-6

To the members of the Deadbeat Club
1970-1973

Judy Furman, Robin Hartmann,
Melanie Barr and
Ruth Ivy Bollinger (1954-1987)

spirit to spirit
I have been to Paris since we parted

And for Mira-Lani Bernard,
Editor, *Von Ryan's Daughter*

They say the devil's water
It ain't so sweet
You don't have to drink right now
But you can dip your feet
Every once in a little while.

The Killers
"When You Were Young"

I went out to the hazel wood
Because a fire was in my head.

Yeats
"Song of the Wandering Aengus"

I

1.

Far, far out in the foothills is where the lightning begins, just a flicker, a spilling of silver in the dark rock and unmoving bundles of cloud. Then it comes forward, daddy long legs, its own long swinging threads of light its only light. It is up at the edge of the town, the third or fourth flash, before Hadley hears the boom the first one made. Then another flash as new booms come, then more booms, an echoing.

It is like the Blake poem in her poetry book: the chorus (she thinks it is a song more than anything) going *And all the hills echoed,* three syllables to "echoed," the last one stressed. *Boom. Boom.*

The little spots of roofs at the edge of town light up. There was supposed to have been more building by now, streets and streets with so many houses there would have to be new lanes made and cul-de-sacs, but the building never happened, it never came this far. The roofs and sidings lay there now like confetti from a never-happened celebration.

The valley where her family lives was supposed to be the next, most natural place for the city to grow. The aerospace companies were going to build new factories here. The city couldn't go south without blending into San Diego, and East of the freeways was all built out already, glass and two-lane blacktop unrolling like a hungry tongue out through the miles of dust. People were supposed to be getting used to driving a half-hour, an hour, then an hour and a half to work and back again. Everything was in place here in this newest, this emptiest of spaces.

The people came. The new roads came. The stores that gave them food and phones and cheap designer clothes: They were here or would come. A radio station. A TV station.

But a crimp, a ripple, a whatever-they-call-it hit all of aerospace just as they were planning Hadley's graduation party six years ago. Everything slowed, wound down. And when things started up again, they started slower, got going slower, the spaces of time between things stretching out. They would see trucks parked along the ridges by the new buildings. They waited for more building to start. But the men getting out of their trucks would be taking *down* signs, unfastening propane tanks. Then the moving trucks would come, and the streets would be full of wardrobe boxes as big as cars, as big, it seemed, as some of the roofs of the buildings themselves.

Then the houses were empty, or if they were not empty, their people would not leave in the morning or return in the evening. It became like a movie set: which parts were real and which were not became confusing. Maybe, they thought, it was fitting that it could all go hollow and empty like a set, like a mirage, an illusion. This was the city that got started by making such things for the world. *Don't worry, don't worry* another poem in her book says. *It is only a movie, it is only a beam of light.*

Crack comes a closer flash of it. *Crack* comes a flash closer still. The long and spindly fire-feet are walking down the valley sides and up the streets. It is like a Frankenstein's lab. The levers are being pulled. The great assembled monster is sleeping, waiting to be juiced. The knobs on its neck are thirsty for electrons.

In the brightest flash Hadley sees it, down in the old garages at the center of town. A ball of fire all on its own, carried along by running feet.

2.

"Lena's daughter got burned bad," Hadley's mother says, whipping the eggs, watching a tiny rope of smoke rise up from the toaster. She sits a plate in front of Hadley and one in front of herself, and starts with The Stare.

"I mean, burned *bad*. Third degree. Whole upper body. And it burned off her hair."

Hadley looks out the window and her father's car is gone. Her mother is buoyant today, *chipper*, because she knows he has work. She gets giddy-chatty.

"All to make a little money," she says.

The toast pops up and Hadley says nothing.

Her mother knows nothing, not *squat*, not anything, about crank. She only says "using" because she got it out of some recovering addict's speech in a newspaper. Otherwise she would say "taking" or, worse, "smoking," or something else you don't do with it.

She's trolling with me, Hadley thinks, like all the mothers here. They cared less about your encounters with sex, with money, with when the hell you'll get out of here, with your health, with your hair or whether you're eating enough lunch, with how you're doing at school, with rabid animals and the drag racing everybody is doing out on 395, than they do about crank. It's because that's all anybody pays attention to in this place now. It's the only thing that makes them newsworthy to anybody but economists or mad scientists, Hadley thinks. Geologists.

Actually, there's lots more here that gets written up. Traditional-type outlaws that take hostages and kill and dismember snitches. The new country music arena, Sweet Voice, built over by the Outlet Mall. But crank is what Hadley's mother is reading about. What the news programs have on them. And what she thinks Hadley might actually bite off on and get roped into. Never mind sex slavery or eating disorders. It's all *boil boil, toil and trouble* now. What happens in the labs is what they are.

And the girl—Lena's daughter—did almost die. The paper said layers and layers of skin.

"It's the water that you lose, what kills you with burns." Hadley's mother wanted to be a nurse, or even a doctor, but lost too much time (she says) putting Hadley's father through school. Burns seem to be her specialty: the idea that flesh could do that, as much as paper or wood.

"She ran too far, is what they said. You can't give that stuff any air. It's like the jet fuel on the buildings in 9/11. You've got to snuff it out."

Hadley puts a long trail of jam, thin as a snail's path, across her toast.

"Stop, drop and roll," she says.

"This isn't funny, Hadley."

"I'm not *being* funny." Hadley's mother has no sense of humor when crank-trolling. She is in her chops, *owning* her interrogation. Swimming in it like a fish in water. She is one with it.

"You better just…." She let out a long sigh. "You better just be a friend to her now. Just be there for her."

If Hadley's mother knows anything, it's that softening Hadley up like this won't do it. And she knows that Hadley is onto her lingo and her would-be reasoning. Hadley can spot the women's magazine lines.

"I'll try," Hadley says earnestly, not a vestige of sarcasm.

She has never really known Natasha Varvouchka well. Their family were hard-core New Russians. They had come here from Brooklyn, Odessa, places they led others to believe were really the same place. Natasha's cousin, Misha, had been one of the guys robbing the bank in North Hollywood a couple years back, the ones with body armor and so much firepower that the cops fighting them had to go into the local gun store to up their weaponry. And they were pure Russians, not Armenian-Russians, like so many of the families here.

     RICHARD WIRICK

The digital numbers on the clock radio show quarter till. Hadley is saved by the bus. Both she and her mother hear its groaning in the hills: bad gears, bad exhaust. The school district has no taxes, no money, no way to really run an institution of any kind for them. "Better than being locked up," Hadley's father said. "Besides, it doesn't matter where you go to junior college." That is her father, believer in miracles. His miracle, his raising himself up into something like the chapel-ceiling Adam he saw once but whispers about to Hadley always, "One finger the First Finger," he says. And she sees it: moistened and bent in the trickles of cloud.

Hadley kisses her mother goodbye, avoiding her own hooded eyes, and takes some wetted napkins to wipe the dust off the bus seat.

3.

Hadley is twenty-three. People wonder about all the things she knows, and it's true she was a brainiac early on, checking eight or ten books out a week, starting in about middle school, from the hot, small, well-meaning library over in Acton. A lot of what she chose was based on covers, the art on the Penguin classics, like Beatrice holding the white flower out to Dante on the front of *The New Life.* It was small, *thin.* It fit in a jacket pocket. She tried to keep them thin and portable: *Dubliners* instead of *A Portrait, Songs of Innocence* rather than the fatter books of his with bearded Biblical figures and compasses and wheels. She got a lot, always, in her pockets, at least two books in each. And one book led to another, like "Indian Camp" in *In Our Time*, when the Chippewa father cuts his own throat in the bunk above the one his newest baby is being born in—that made her curious about abortion and Canada and boat propellers all at the same time. So she was thinking about boats and checked out a long essay, taking up a whole book, by John McPhee, called *The Survival of the Birch Canoe.* Things like that.

Then birches, just that type of tree. That led to Russia, to all its buggy-eyed saints and revolutions, and the strange alphabet she would stare at on banners in old photographs. Usually by the light of the TV. Falling asleep.

That's the other thing, television. So much more of what she has in her head is from TV, especially after they got the wide screen from the Sautters when they lost their house. So, so much from TV. Her mother said they called it a wasteland in her day, but Hadley loves the hundreds of channels: ten for history, ten for nature, maybe fifteen about people's lives. She knows more sometimes about her Mom and Dad's years growing up, what was happening to the country in the 60s and 70s, than they do. And it's from surfing the channels, by herself at night, those hundreds of windows opening, one into another, all at her fingertips. *"I am a creature of this medium,"* somebody on one of the shows said. She is. That's her. Some of the junk, the TMZ stuff, she likes too—the humor, the *irony*, the so-stupid-you-have-to-watch-it wicked comical sneering of the hosts.

Then back into the History Channel: Tanks rolling in grey, grainy, treeless streets when her Mom was her age. One small Chinese kid in a square, standing in front of one.

Professor Tolles could tell right away how much TV she knew. That, as much as the books, is what sunk into her writing, and that's what makes Hadley think he's eyeing her, thinking of plucking her out for the school journal's masthead.

She is 23 and she is stuffing herself with all this knowledge, like packing going into a box. She lifts the flaps and it falls in. Like the styrofoam peanuts and strips of newsprint. All of it is remembered. Every piece is taken and claimed. All of it makes her happy and brave. And like you learn from the History Channel, for people like Hadley, in places like this, it is the way out, the way loose. The way away.

4.

As dirty as it is, sometimes Hadley likes riding the bus. It's the way "Napoleon Dynamite" opens, with Napoleon trying to just hang out and the kid asking what he was going to do that day, and then when the kid bothers him, Napoleon unwraps the little parachute man and drops him out the window to drag across the road, a dust road like this one.

Jed is three or four seats up ahead. His band is the one she hears across the allotment on Thursday nights, a jerking-up-and-down and crashing sound, like the movers that are always coming in and then going out. He acts like he doesn't know she's there, but Jemma told her he's sweating her bad. "*Bad*," Jemma had said, tilting her head forward in the Girls' room mirror and using the comb handle to find her part. "Let me see if he can find something better than my girl." Jemma put the comb in her teeth and gathered her hair together fast, so quick you couldn't see her hands. Her purse was open beside the sink, sky blue, with feathers made out of a carton of American Spirit cigarettes.

Hadley wants to play eye-fuck bad with Jed, with him having to do all the looking around, but really all she can see is her mother's face froze the way it was when Hadley kissed her, like dough about to collapse, the air inside it seeping out through its cracks.

* * *

Hadley was the one who'd found her mother that day. She could tell something was wrong, the way her hand was lying stretched straight out, and the color of her skin. "Waxen" is the way it is described in books. And the way Hadley pushed her hard, pressed down on that hand and down hard on her head until she heard the groan that she knew would come. *No matter what color they are, if there's a noise they're still alive.*

It seemed like years since that morning, but it has only been a couple of months. None of that happening, none of that almost dying, none of it changed her. People are supposed to get enlightened by things like that, come to big realizations. All that right there up in your face, eons and eons of blankness. None of it changes anything. You go on being what you were, as if you'd been born as a rock.

The crowds of haze rise up over the hill ahead and light streams through, like a searchlight, that strong. When Hadley wipes her skin, the grime makes a stream on her arm.

But she's happy. Jed is looking back her way, saying something to whoever is sitting next to him about how fine she is.

5.

Being stuck here in school, Antelope Valley Community College, is something Hadley could write about all by itself, but what is mostly on everybody's mind while they're there is the heat. It's like she has read the heat is in Africa. It is thick and still, like a wall. Nothing moves in it. It can be full of smells, but it has a smell itself, which seems nothing more than its thickness, the smell of the hardness and slowness of going through it. And the wake you make with your body, or a hand or paper you fan yourself with, seems just the same as it, not much more than mixing it around.

It kills things. Wild dogs in the road. Bugs all over the walkways between buildings, dried like fallen leaves with their legs cocked and their antennae spread out like flower stems. And old people die in it, too. People on the porch of the home, walking on its grounds. People in folding chairs and parades. The Boy Scouts and Campfire Girls standing at attention don't die, but they faint, and the sound of them crashing down is like a toolbox falling, a box of cans dropping out of the back of a station wagon.

In class, it is too hot to talk or think. It is too hot to listen, because the heat is what you're thinking about. The teachers go through a lot of handkerchiefs, wiping their faces. Sometimes they stop and lean their hands against the wall. The fans don't make any difference. *A bellows in hell.* Blake again. It isn't hell here, but besides the city below being squeezed out and overpopulated, you wonder, on these hot, hot afternoons, why the place they were standing in was ever settled.

Jed comes up behind her at her locker. His breath makes the hair on the back of her neck stand up straight in the heat, the puff of it like breeze through grass, that sweet and cool feeling. He says he's heard Natasha is getting better and will be out of the hospital in maybe a week. He had seen her mother, Lena, at Best Buy. All of the grafts had worked; they had "taken" well and only had to be done on parts of her body that could be covered by clothes.

Hadley wants Jed to pull her back into him, put his mouth on the top of her head so his own hair will fall around hers. "Jungle Fever" he calls it, the hair mixing up, looping around like noodles in heating soup. But people, teachers, would see. In high school they called it PDA—Public Display of Affection. They still fuck you for that in this place. It was the same thing for her father and mother in the Seventies, down in the city. "*The job of love*," her mother calls relationships sometimes. Sometimes hiding it was half the work.

Jed runs his hand along her sword tattoo, tracing the barbed wire that twines around its blade. He and some friends are going to see Natasha at Antelope Memorial on Thursday. Jemma would come, J.T. and some people in his band, Jed's sister Olivia and her boyfriend, Dean, who looks strangely like Jed.

When Hadley shuts her locker, the clammy blast of it goes down the hall like jail doors slamming in the movies. The weakening last flat echoes of the locker's double metal latches, then the voices of all the rooms around them start up, the classroom doors open, a couple sets of feet slap down the stairs.

6.

In her room that night, Hadley thinks of going to see Natasha. They can visit her on Thursday and on Saturday morning Natasha will be out. The burns are from ephedra blasts, explosions that sometimes happen when the flames in a lab get too high or the compound base is uneven.

Hadley doesn't know why, when they are running a batch, they don't cover themselves with big thick cloaks or jackets. They don't have to be fire suits like the drivers wear at the Pomona drags, but they need something with a hood, a big hood that can be pulled around to cover the face completely if a pot lid blew.

Ephedra compound is horrible, a kind of sticky oil that flattens thinly across whatever it hits and carries the fire with it to whatever it touches. Only a few other things in nature are like it, that *determined*, that made to destroy. Jet fuel is one, with its base of kerosene. It's what made the fires so hot and terrible when the planes hit the towers in New York, the smoke pitch black and tumbling out the windows, multiplying itself by the seconds.

Pictures of kids from the Valley are in the papers all the time, in magazines like *Time* and *The Economist*. They are like scarred little children caught sleeping in a burning house, the skin stretched and gummed up not so much from the flames as from the unbelievable heat in the room, the way flesh just starts, like anything else, to boil, to soften and roast. People who picked little kids like that up saw their cheeks and necks melt before their eyes, sheets of tiny features collapsing like fruit in the garbage. Molecules shouldn't be going that fast, at least not in anything living.

When skin like that heats up, it is like paint that has already started to dry when you start to spread it. There are bubbles and mottles and pits surrounded by flaps and ridges and little ice-like craters of tissue. It is a burn doctor's laboratory; it was seventh heaven for Hadley's failed nurse-mother's fire obsessions.

There are the before and after pictures you see in color in the warning stories in *Newsweek*. Smooth-skinned 4H-ers gone to acne vulgaris, to hemangioma in one faulty boom. Firefighters and racers, the test pilots they saw at bars over at Edwards who looked like this. But they have their bravery to blame. It's a red badge of something. Batch cookers have nothing, *nada*. A botched life, a face like a black mountainside.

Hadley crawls out the gable window in her track suit and lights a spliff. Fire, fire is on her mind, and she imagines the ashes from her joint sparking the two or three old slopes of shingles, one on top of the other, that her father let sometimes stoned, sometimes scarred young roofers lay over the years. Everyone wears their traces of fire. Everyone walks with the fire inside.

She sees the half moon staring down at itself in the catch pools of the gravel pit. It has dropped a silver dust over the cactuses and the whale-backed roof of the mall's four-plex. All across the Valley she can see uneven lights flickering in the trailer and bunkhouse windows. In this land without fireplaces or woodstoves, without anything else that it could be, little trails of white drift up from all sides into space out of the silver chimney pipes, the whole hillside of them working like a silent church organ.

7.

Jed is in front of her walking down the hospital corridor, the two of them in a long trail of maybe eight or twelve, people Hadley would think twice about letting in if she were an adult and ran a hospital like this. A bunch of kids in the burn unit must seem strange to the nurses. But maybe not with all the phedra fires all of it going, going all the time.

Like a long centipede or Chinese dragon, they turn to the right, Will leading them with his huge squiggly basket of hair arched up like a banana or half-moon, funny how it grows only sideways and not up. His four fan-club girls follow him. Jed and Hadley call them the Sisters of Will, Jed saying he is waiting for them to etch "W's" in their foreheads. Two kids they don't know have come, friends of Natasha's sister, Ada.

And then they are in the room. It is big enough to fit all of them, no second bed or curtain in the middle. This has to be one of those hospitals that never has enough patients and starts advertising, but here it probably doesn't even do that, just lays waiting for the next truck or bush-hog crash, or the next bunch of cookers.

Natasha's doctor, dark-skinned with fine black hair, smiles at them as he leaves. His name tag has the longest word after doctor, with "angs" and "abands" echoing in black etched letters across the white plastic.

Natasha is white, wrapped like a mummy with slits for her eyes. Her arms are clear, untouched by the flames. Everybody mills around except Jed, who pulls himself up beside the bed and stands respectfully, like a soldier, smiling down and waiting for her to say something. When her thick accent comes out from under the gauze, like a rapid metal tapping, Hadley has to look to her eyes to see what it

     RICHARD WIRICK

is—a joke, a complaint or question. Hadley can't tell. She will ask Jed later.

Behind the pair we don't know Hadley sees a small woman with black spiked hair biting her nails. It is Lena, Natasha's mother, who at first won't look at them at all but then finally starts staring at the girls one by one. The girls seem to break apart, the pairs of them splitting in the ray-glare of her narrow, bushy-browed slits. When there is no one between them, the eyes are on Hadley, little coals, tiny sparks. How can she blame her daughter lying there? It has to be someone. And here they have come, her strange American friends.

* * *

Hadley watches their line again on the way out, and sees the Sisters of Will eyeing the cabinets, rubber-necking over the bright-lit stocked and congested nurses' station for open units of packages and vials. Their heads cock up when orderlies pass with tiny white cups of pills and capped glasses with bent straws. Hadley can almost see the hunger glowing in their eyes through the backs of their heads, scoping out the tops of walls and shelves and lockless, digital-combinated cupboards.

And then Jed, just ahead of her, starts to do it too. The burn goes up out of Hadley's heart and spreads through her neck and under her chin. She whispers his name, and then she starts to softly say, "No… no," and then stops. Why should she think it of him? Why shouldn't she? All the way home, the knowledge lies between them in the dark back seat. She won't go over to him. She watches the lights of the towns fly over the hood of the SUV and spin in J.T.'s and the others' hair, and lets the light rise up her lap and over her face and then jump to Jed.

But it doesn't take on Jed. Nothing lays on him, nothing sticks to him. He is like a black hole, Hadley thinks, the Lord of Gravity. The quick columns of brightness fall down into him, disappearing. He could be home. He could be anywhere but here.

8.

Hadley's father has the hangdong, poor-puppy look his face gets after a talk with Hadley's mother when he is working. When he doesn't have a gig, the look is worse, like she has whipped him or driven over his feet, or else they don't talk at all and he sits in his office or out at the garage workbench listening to satellite radio. Hadley loves him when he is like this, firm and satisfied and standing up to her mother. It's the condition he wears best, the skin he feels most himself in.

But he's worried after Natasha, and, for Hadley, it's like sitting with her mother all over again. She can push the questions away sometimes by getting interested in his drafting, getting him to talk about it. He'll sketch the dimensions in the air, thumbs and fingers flying around his sandy hair. And she'll ask a question about something like the B-1, and a hush will come into his voice, an echoey spell, letting Hadley know he has worked on something almost close to holy.

"Is she out yet? Natasha?"

Hadley swings her feet around and puts them against the lower part of one of his legs.

"I don't know her that well."

"I'm *proud* of you, honey. It was the right thing to do."

The creases of worry around his eyes are lost in shadow, and the glimmer of his pupils fills with the shades of the air too, and Hadley's fear of what they'll see in her, or make her say, bring the giant planes to mind again, new questions she could ask about them: dimensions, velocity.

Her mother sees her father as weak, someone lucky to get the drafting casuals old Lockheed friends slip to him. Somebody lucky to have her, somebody who should be grateful she hasn't thrown him out yet.

"Well, I'm sure she's happy you came, " he says. "Whatever your relationship beforehand. The world's changed for her now."

He won't prod more, Hadley knows. And she thinks it's because he realizes she may listen, may actually follow what he says. They are the only human words, besides maybe Jed's, that could make her do anything, or think about doing anything now. What anyone else tells her, she sees as pushing her toward another life, her life lived by somebody else. She's not certain why, but what he says would be the opposite of that. What he says, she could take into what she is.

His hands lay flat on his upper legs now, the long fingers wrapped down around his khakis. In moments like these there is little Hadley knows but that she loves him. She sees his hands moving along the tilted plank of square paper under the small lamp in a room of shade like this one, leaving behind the lines and planes that will slowly, over weeks and months and years, turn into great machines.

9.

Waiting for the bus to school today, she saw a DEA van come for the couple who live in the place above Blockbuster. She could tell DEA by the windbreakers, a lighter blue than the Navy-colored jackets ATF or Sheriffs wear. Drug men usually have suits underneath, natty, dark and groomed up like the TV Land "Untouchables" of old. They are like that, like FBI. They look like they have just had to leave their desks or a business appointment for the bothersome, headachey dirty work of actually having to do something in the field. They look like they only have enough time to be making the bust they're dispatched on, just that window, and that everything has to stay on script so they can get back to their still-warm cups of coffee.

One man, the captain, stands toward the rear like the cop up on a berm in a traffic stop. His jacket bulges out in back with the hard angles of an automatic pistol, one with a heavy magazine if all hell breaks loose. A couple of sergeants bang on the door. A third sergeant has the warrant in a yellow-tinted plastic envelope the color of pee. The breeze whips the folder cover into a flutter, that metal ratcheting sound like the sides of the storage sheds in a strong wind. The man places his hand on it to make it stop. The captain feels around behind him and touches the bulge, runs his finger along the column of the barrel hidden under the *zip* sound of the rayon. Then he adjusts the pistol he has on his belt, which has a badge on the top flap of its holster. They all wear reflector sunglasses, oversized, like the celebutantes on VH1. They have clean, full, ungreased hair, one of them blond, not the brush cuts you expect from CSI shows.

There are so many like the Blockbuster couple that Hadley has a hard time remembering them now. They are Romanians, themselves very young, from orphanages in its capital city, who were abandoned after the fall of the country. They grew up in the streets of the city, one street she remembers from a documentary called "Little Money Street"— "Little" as in "No." Packs of them ran together, running scams where they distracted visitors with newspapers until one of the smaller ones could come around and lift out a wallet, jerk away a purse. They were dark-skinned, and the cameramen thought them Black Sea people, *people of color*. They at first thought they were gypsies, "Roma," many of whom lived in Romania anyway. But the darkness was just dirt. It was the grime of life with your face turned up at the sun all the time, sleepless and never washing, splattered with the much of food thrown out the back of ministry kitchens for which they have stood all morning waiting.

When they were children, they tore up rags and dipped them in Toluene, a solvent that got them high with the fumes that mixed the chemical with their own perspiration and saliva. "Toli Rags," they called them, and on the grainy film, Hadley had seen packs of kids sharing them, ripping them up and breaking them down even more, into little squares. Before the running camera, they stood or walked or crouched, holding the rags over their noses. Some of them had the smaller rags inhaled over their noses, stuck to them in contests to see who could hold it up the longest. After a few minutes they would wobble in front of the lens, fall over, fall down in groups.

Hadley is assuming the Blockbuster couple were Toli kids, but it is a safe assumption. The only other way they would have gotten a habit would have been as government people's children, with access to heroin and synthetic opiates that became one of the means of exchange in the twilit time between the Big Man's fall and whatever government they have there now. Maybe they were just that. It made getting out easier. You could get your visa and drift from club to club through the capitals of Europe until you were out, really out. A true street kid had to smuggle himself, ride in plane wheel casings or in ships' containers.

Hadley knows that the man had gotten disabled on a punch press, making Saturday night specials in one of the little mall factories in Lake Elsinore. His Kaiser doctor got him Oxycontin, a limited scrip, only for a short time, blah-blah, and that was it. They tumbled back into all of it. The streets of Bucharest came back to gobble them up, to fumble over them with its gums and tongue. They were buying green monsters —20 milligram Oxy capsules—from kids here in the Valley at $80 a pop. The sellers were using the money to finance their crank biz, and the buyers, including Mr. and Mrs. Bucharest, started to live for it. It took the place of oxygen and light and food. It was larger than their life and anything in it. It was larger than love.

They had a three-year-old kid, a girl. Sometimes they took her to the park and you could see them twirling her on one of those spinning platforms that look like a Lazy Susan. After their habit started they didn't come out of the house. They didn't open windows or go out to the market. The dust built up on their car and their antennae fell over, its flat wire gone slack. Birds started to live in crevices above their screen door. The grass grew and when tree limbs fell into their yard, no one picked them up. Cops would sit in their cars outside. Hadley knew they were watching them and not Blockbuster. But nothing happened, nothing came of it.

Then the little girl died. She ate one of the capsules that had fallen on the carpet. Even with an adult, Oxy can stop the heart for long, terrible seconds. It has that kind of power. The respiratory system crashes, falls down like under a blast of wind. The father and mother were trying to revive her when 911 came in and found the three of them on the carpet in the living room. Right where she had eaten it. The baby had fallen over as soon as she picked it out of the carpet and swallowed it. The lungs switched off. She was blue before the parents walked out of the den and found her.

The two sergeants without the warrant talk between themselves and try to decide something. Then one of them goes back to the van and carries a megaphone, white with a red tapering mike, up to the living room picture window. He stops, looks down, swings the thing between his hands. He looks for a minute like he may lift it up and break the window with it. He takes it back to the van and when he walks back toward his partner, he has started to snap open his holster.

The bus comes up over the hill and, as the men close up around the door, they have their guns in their right hands. The captain leaves

RICHARD WIRICK

the machine pistol alone and has his sidearm up. The warrant is folded in the newspaper hook under their mailbox, black with a little gold eagle on it, its wings spread, like something you would see on a badge or on the back of money, the four of them are frozen there, like plaster lawn sculptures, those little walking families of deer.

When the bus stops, brakes hissing, the horrible white elderly dialysis transport doors opening, Hadley climbs up and walks back her usual four rows. *Four corners, four winds.* She doesn't take her eyes off the men as they start to yell out their orders. But it is all just noise under the bus sounds. She can't hear anything they are saying.

No one comes to the door. And though she knows better, the bus driver, curious, stays stopped, her door open, acting like she is waiting for somebody else to run up and get in.

After the long minutes, with the men looking like they are about to just kick in and sweep the place, the door pulls back and the shadows of the living room close over the white. At first Hadley can't see anything in the doorway. Then the small head starts to materialize behind the screen. It's not the mother or father, but somebody else, somebody younger, looking to be a tall twelve-year-old, or young teen. Maybe a cousin or neighbor who came to help after the little girl's funeral. She or he, Hadley can't really tell which with the slender build and spiked hair, stands talking to them for a minute or two, then steps back from the door as it opens. The last man in picks up the warrant, still rolled into a tube, and puts it in his back pocket.

As the bus starts rolling, Hadley pulls out her Blake and sees the Gilded One standing in his column of fire, couplets racing along under him as if they were clouds he is standing on. She remembers something. The parents went on as normally as they could after their daughter died. Neither of them went back to work, but they wouldn't have been able to anyway with the way their habits were going. They had been tagged by an undercover man, maybe caught on a surveillance tape, for something involving the baby's clothes. It was her pants and shoes and a snowsuit they were trying to sell, for more pills.

10.

Jed and the others are cooking a batch today, starting early, before any of the stores or diners open. It's Bob's, Jed's cousin's place that they use, just off the main access road to the 395 interchange. There can be highway patrol here anytime really, but they tend to keep their cars pointed toward the four-lane, waiting for unplated Mexicans and speeding truckers. They tend to be sleeping, to tell you the truth. Jed says that those of them who get up that early and peek into their cruisers can tell you.

Hadley is just watching. She wouldn't go near any of the stuff, not with a ten-foot pole. She never even liked burning trash for her father back when it was still legal. She is not a fire girl. She is a water girl.

Jed's other cousin, Baker, brings in the half-gallon jugs of Ephedrine with the Gatorade labels still on. The E- powder is in water that's tinted the same shade as Gatorade, in case they get stopped. With the purchase limits on cold medicines, Baker and his crew have to sweep a couple of counties to get enough powder from caplets. They've had to go east into Kern and Fresno counties, staying just ahead of the Sheriff Departments' computers.

As Baker's boys come in, Hadley can hear the stuff—ambrosia, they call it—sloshing around in the jugs, four of them nestled onto a leather platform running around Baker's military jacket, held up with a canvas harness. The guys behind him wear the same rig, all of them sloshing, sloshing, like the lake water on the Salton beaches. And the sloshes themselves echo, back and forth, a whispery sound.

Others come out from the back rooms with the cooker pots and stills and wire tubing, all of this group wearing asbestos headgear in case of a blow, in case of what Natasha had the bad cards to be next

    RICHARD WIRICK

to. The suits have little pointed hoods that look like bat heads, or the burlap hoods they put on condemned men, and their shoulder pads rise up too, like little wings.

Hadley thinks this must be Gulf War gear; it has that kind of brown and yellow camo patching, desert colors.

And then, with all the grounds and tubes connected and the mixtures double-checked, one of them, a rookie you can bet, steps forward to light the burner, and that's that.

"The Mole People," Jed calls them when they work like this, and Hadley sees that it does all have an under-the-earth rhythm, full of muted subterranean stinks and bangs, and chilly, tinkering, maze-like clinkings.

They sit back on their boxes and somebody slips in a tape, Allman Brothers, always them, or Lynyrd Skynyrd: bands before Hadley's times, before the times, even, of her friends' older brothers and sisters. None of these guys have iPods; the world stopped for them twenty years ago. They light cigarettes as the song goes: *TIED to a whippin' post. TIED to a whippin' post*, over and over.

Hadley thinks how all men do their work this way. The business of the world done all in hidden places, in the dark and cold, places you would not want to bring someone to. Especially this place, especially here. All of it, the final product, ending up in the bodies of kids who decide to fall, to sidestep the world, looking for a way to make their slippage dramatic—to give it a rapid, jittery swiftness. It is as natural as leaves searching for the sun, this thirst for a way to skate through, no, to barrel like a rocket through the senseless emptiness, the long stretches of dead time.

She watches them tapping on their jeans as the music plays, the fire under the pots and the fluids rising through the tubes. It is like a riddle, this collection of things. It is like a Sphinx sitting on a column in an ancient place, something whose questions they'll answer, with the answer giving them power.

A coal flickers out from one of the burners and Baker's guy gets it, stomps on it.

The big buyers now, Hadley knows, are mothers, maybe five years older than she is, with kids they thought would excite their lives but that became such a job, tugging at them, hanging on and slowing them down, puppies latched onto the nipples of dogs as they try to get up and change position in the sun.

Hadley thinks of people at the beginning of life, the new users. And the ones whose beginning is already underway, is rolling—the mothers. If you get people at those two moments of time, those frozen moments, those snapshots, you will have everyone. The stuff sinks into you. You think you are the falconer, *who cannot hear*, and the falcon sticks its talons through your gloves. It fastens to you like the liquid fire on the building's sides, the atoms in their electrified racing—fire in the blood, electric blood. It boils away structure, boils away posture, the bones of your body's floors and pulleys and ladders collapsing.

The mothering will stop, maybe completely. The ones who do have babies are having them taken away. You can end things this way, whole small populations, entire swaths of a town. And these guys— Baker's boys—see no other path for themselves, no other way to make it so surely and easily.

Steam has filed the air, beads of water hanging on every still thing in the room. Their glasses, their chins. The little plastic window of the cassette player.

Baker pushes the fast forward until the tape turns over into what she knows will be slower tunes, ballads and anthems. This is the music to which the stuff will harden, returning to powder. There is nothing to do now but wait.

11.

Every time she's not able to sleep, when she's resting on Jed's chest and he's been asking her the hard questions of how much of the crank trade he should be involved in—all good questions, all impossible, the hardest kind of decisions in the world—and she can't listen to any of it anymore, and there's no chance of shaking it off, she tries in her mind to retrace the maps. They are terrain plates of the Valley and its surrounding mountains, and Hadley checks them out of the library along with her poetry books.

They are published by the Geology Service, and unfold from small plastic squares into great creased posters of ripples and contours and swales, each in a different color and spotted with same-colored tiny "Ts" and flecks that lie under each circle and tapered crenellation like a hillside full of crosses. The maps tell the story of this place's formation in the Ice Age, of why it is a place of stone and sand rather than topsoil and greenery. It is the story of great forces underneath what you see, and which she imagines can be forces still—pulling the mind to a deeper place than the ticks and strains and clutter that trap it up here in the blue where they live.

Hadley's father taught her to read the colors; he'd gotten the maps from government men for whom he'd done casuals. He smooths them out with his long arms when he sits her down at his table, the wide white tear sheet filled with yellow, ovoid lamplight. Where most draftsmen might only point, he taps each thing he talks about, his nails clicking against the plastic, like a minister tapping the lectern, creating and arranging.

The colors tell the stories: "Brighter than the historian's are the mapmaker's colors."

The yellow patches were lakes or swamps, really the sand surrounding them, in rolled, cupped banks of ridges and gently sloping dry strands. All through these gold and cream and other-colored circles are triangles—drumlins, the geographers call them—that stand for hills of different consistencies that held the sand surfaces together and hedged the flows of ice.

Groups of green and purple rings wobble across each other and taper away like smoke or serpent's tails. The green trails are eskers, tiny humpbacked mountains that signal like deaf hands the routes of rivers that cut under the ice, running as constant and cool as spring streams. They were big, gushing shotgun blasts of gravel and slush, and they left behind shadows of themselves, little creeks or ditches that lie at the edge of the once wide path.

The purple trails, more hidden, more *quiet*, are the end moraines, where the ice stopped, a hundred years here and a hundred years there, leaving boulder walls and quarries of egg-smooth dusted stone.

There are pink and red strokes that come up like rosy heater's coils, but are no more than the cliffs and sharper banks of lakes that were once twenty, forty, a hundred miles across. The pastel *rosas*, as bright a pink as sidewalk chalk, are limestone striations and soggy clay and sometimes shale. This is the faultless clock the miles of moving ice imprinted, the soil's skeleton, the bones of the land. The grey swales are soil shards, like ashes left from the roaring of the glacier's engines. But it is a pasty, tilting, gumbo of infertile loam, nothing anybody can raise anything in. No good for crops. Nothing giving the green of the leaf.

Glaciers would fall apart and separate, like any powerful, unorganized thing. The spaces between what was once their drifting chunks are a mocha, cocoa color, called kame moraines. They are scattered, crumbly and wild, the opposite of the drumlins that stayed so smooth and constant and clean. The kame moraines take over from end moraines, the shallows of lavender deepening into burgundy, wine-colored crayons where the rock-filled ice broke apart to stand still for centuries, ossifying, hardening.

Jed dozes off and wakes up again. Hadley can follow the patterns of it in the way his chest moves against her face. Sometimes he'll say her name and she knows, if she answers, he'll want to start the crank talk again—should I do this and who should I believe, how much should I let myself know—and so she stays quiet, playing possum, with her hand unmoving on his belly.

Not for a minute does she stop thinking about the colors blooming up out of the black of her closed eyes. He gives up asking. She feels the edges of his ribs. His body is like the smooth and warming plains of the new-made planet, and her deep and even breathing is the moist and damper air, rising and falling in that first night on Earth.

12.

When the batch is done, they come back. Jed has pretty much made up his mind to move some of it, "ferry" it, as they say. A ferryman does lots of things: breaks down powder bricks from the cooking vats, cuts and weighs them, wraps them in cellophane, keeps the computer logs. He Mapquests directions to major suppliers. He spots new mules, and who could, in turn, be mules for them.

Jed calls all the stuff he would do the "middle work." It puts you out at the edge of things and doesn't really count as being in the business. You aren't making it and you aren't selling it. You are doing something else and something someone would be doing anyway. It's passing through your hands in a way that makes it not matter what it is, or as if it were something else.

This is where he gets Hadley's stare, her hairy eyeball. Watching the Cook the way they did the day before is her idea of middle work. Middle work has got to be not touching. It can't involve any contact. Basically, it shouldn't be anything more than watching. And Hadley likes to think that even this was too much, that she needed to draw the line at something like thinking about it.

She tries to make this point like she does in most of their talking, especially after he's ripped into her for all the guilt-tripping. She points to people who have completely changed now, once they've gotten in further. There is a look about them, especially the women, when they pass her in the parking lots and market aisles. It is where they always are. There is a sameness to them, their hair and eyes, once they've let go and rolled over, once it has all pulled them under.

The other day they were at Home Depot looking for light bulbs. Hadley was nestled down into Jed's jacket, his arm around her the way she likes it when they walk along. She made him stop just before the fork-lift turnaround, in the section where lumber and sheetrock are stacked so high you have to pick them by camera from monitors down at ground level, and get one of the hard hat guys to get it for you.

Mrs. Ridley was there, standing with her neck cocked up at where pallets reached almost to the roof peak. Her hair stuck straight out on each side and was crusted solid like a pair of stage angel wings. She was wearing an army surplus jacket with black stenciled numbers running vertically up the shoulders. It was something Hadley had never seen her wear before, something too cold-weather for the un-moving air of these high alleys of hardware.

It wasn't clear to Hadley what Mrs. Ridley was looking at, if she was looking at anything. She'd gotten a tic, a strange wink that seemed to start under her eye and move up to it, slowly, then more rapidly as she strained to look forward. The side of her face was wet with something and she moved her hand up to itch the other palm. But other than this she didn't move. She was frozen. Perfectly still. Perfectly silent. Hadley motioned to Jed to come closer to her so she wouldn't have to be alone when they passed her. In the little wake of air their walking made, Mrs. Ridley's smell rose up and stung them, strong as battery acid or ammonia, but full of age and earth and earthly creatures, like the wet coat of a dog.

13.

Mrs. Ridley was Hadley's homeroom teacher two years ago. The school board heard about her arrest and plea and fired her. Then she was a grocery checker and, after that, started having basket parties for money. After that, who knows. That's when her skin got leathery and her hair started to fan out and thicken, growing a grey-white stuff between it like on the backs of the terraced gobs of hair on Rastafarians. She would be itching every time Hadley saw her, and speaking less, so that scratching seemed to eventually replace her speech, something that lay on top of her mumbling and helped to hide it. Scratching was her "signifier," as Hadley's father would say: one of those phrases he got from a Navy officer's lecture to pilots he had sneaked into at Edwards. It was how Mrs. Ridley wanted them to know her now. Her signal, the attention-call to her suffering.

And her shuffle, her walking stand. There are so many now that are like Mrs. Ridley. Hadley gets them mixed together. If she started, she could go on for days. It would be like a catalog.

* * *

It's not that Hadley wants to marry Jed. She wouldn't want to be tied down like that herself at this age. Once she has the JC credits in and she can go to art school, she might be leaving anyway. She just wishes she could feel him—how to put it?—fastened on her the way he's fastened on all his driving and scheming and dodging the things that are swarming around them. That look of his, you'd think he was a hunted man.

If it's being trapped, the way they all are here, she understands. All of them are being chased that way. It's harder for boys. The girls are supposed to get married and fall into place somehow, work at a church or at a gas station kiosk. But boys like Jed? They have a vice closing in on them. He looks around and sees, in bars a hill or two away, all kinds of guys his age just coming out of law or med school, their lives assembling, settling in. Even kids out of vocational school, trade colleges. They may be up to their eyeballs in debt, but things are starting for them, they are moving forward, *getting traction.*

For boys getting a start as late as Jed, there are only a couple of roads left open. There's minimum wage stores like Best Buy and Wal Mart, where the most he could hope for is to be managing in a few years, picking up his health insurance. There are the gravel pits, the places they swim and see the moon in, but a lot of those gigs have been taken by Cambodian, Laotian kids, the socket-eyed, skinny ones you used to see in the aisles of the 99 cent stores and produce co-ops. He could get into sales, life insurance and retirement products for the old people forced to move out here by the city's prices, but still swimming in money, money they are too afraid to touch until someone smooth comes along. But these are jobs that take polish, and an evening out of Jed's edges that just might be well nigh impossible—new gestures and speech and treatments for the dark circles under his eyes that give him the lost Johnny Depp look Hadley loves, but that are lasting as bar-fight bruises, the kind of tiny vessel bleeding that really just becomes a kind of dark scar hanging there for good. It's a look that is normal out here, but that brands them with good City people.

And the last option is crank. Or dope of some sort. Direct, indirect. All or nothing, the center or the periphery, take your choice.

Lately Hadley has seen something larger and more separate in Jed's loneliness. It is something directed at her, or at any woman he would know, a thing standing between all men and women. They were always, all of them, always and forever told, with and without language, of a boy's and a man's solitude. Hadley's grandmother, her mother's mother Ada, said they were happiest when they were most alone. No need for another, for *an* other, for somebody to be with, she would say. Men were islands, walkers through a woods where other people were like rocks or trees to them, something to be maneuvered around because there is nothing of themselves they would find there.

But people were—what?—to women. More like mirrors, windows, flashing something back or letting the eye go in and roam, go in and learn. Women needed people to situate themselves, and for that reason, just plain *needed* them, needed people. In men, Hadley had been told, there is no need, or none that they admitted.

Jed didn't look at her so much as look around her when he saw her, as if expecting someone else, or waiting for her to turn into something else. Even laying on top of her, spraying his white splash on her, it wasn't her he looked at, but the force, the fire the two of them made together.

So people like Cocteau, whose books Hadley got once and who looked more like a woman than any man—an old woman, a grandmother wearing pancake make-up—Cocteau would say they fitted themselves to others like people in a dream, the visitors completely uninvited and throwing them off their habits but all of them, especially those of them born female, accepting it as something natural, and acting naturally.

Two of the women, the cranked ones, whom Hadley promised herself she would catalog:

Mrs. Dickinson, the minister's wife. After he divorced her she grew very large and then very small, and then after almost six months, Hadley would see the leanness, the hunger around her eyes. She got boils, burn marks on her lips. She slept in the car one night with the window open. A layer of dust thick enough to cover her completely flew in the window and settled on her, an inch deep almost. Now she held up lines at Albertsons with her electronic food stamps, pecking mistaken number connections onto the keypad, the screen blinking, her hissing and stamping and typing the number in again.

And Mrs. McNaul, the nurse from school who came from Valley Regional in Fresno. She started using. It was hard to spot. Then she started stealing other stuff from narcotics closets, saleable stuff like Dilaudid and Fentanyl, until they caught her and she lost her license. This was someone who could calm you, talk you through a panic at-

RICHARD WIRICK

tack, or just help you get rid of your cramps. But she is ruined now, a speedballer, her kids taken away. She drives around town endlessly in her beat-up Mustang, wearing Roy Orbison sunglasses and chewing gum. She mutters, blurts out strange cackles in public places. Bird sounds come up out of her throat even when he mouth is closed, like a Tourette's patient. Hadley has seen Mrs. McNaul pulled over, leaning out the open car door with the dry heaves.

And those are only two. Visitors in a dream. Uninvited, unexpected. But accommodated, invited in to sing in dream voices, small mouse voices, dusty and crushed.

14.

Jed tells Hadley that what he'll be doing now for them is driving a truck, a two-ton panel from their Valley to the next, to a place south of Chatsworth. Van Nuys maybe, Santa Clarita, one of the many no-name swales of shit and Hi-Los and tumbleweed. Each load is one-way, return empty, no unloading, like in the days when unions ruled the world and you couldn't lean over and punch in the cigarette lighter without clearing it with the shop boss.

It is easy work, and it will pay daily or weekly, directly, without Jed's having to coddle to anyone every day as he does it. No having to please anyone, no politics.

And he doesn't know what's inside, ever. He will have a general idea. He will know what it isn't and have some idea of what it might be. There will be a bill of lading that can be made to look like it was supposed to be for something else, other objects or goods, and that will clearly show someone else, not Jed, to be responsible. And the someone else can be made to look, also, like a mistake.

But as to the exact thing, the precise thing he's carrying, it's got to be made to look like he cannot possibly know what it is. Not for that very trip and the load that might be looked at if he's pulled over. He can only know who his supervisor is, and not be privy to every-thing that supervisor—his appointed person, in a position of control Jed would never question—might know, might decide to haul that trip.

"Plausible deniability" was what it was called once, a half-comic, knowing phrase from an Eighties political scandal, cobbled together out of psychology and espionage.

Hadley is sitting with Jed in the basement rec room, going over his Section Four Truck License test manual. She knows he's gotten a

　　　　　　　　RICHARD WIRICK

going-over from his father a while before, a father very different from Hadley's, of the old-fashioned school. He will judge Jed, look at what he's doing and find it falling short, and let Jed hear about it. There would be none of what Hadley finds with her father, none of his approval of everything in advance, the impossibility of Hadley doing anything wrong. With Jed's father everything—even before Jed knows what it is—is wrong, presumed to be wrong, with the son bearing the burden of proving it otherwise.

She loves the way Jed sits, with his knees up under his chin. He looks like a half-weakened, blinking knight. His face says: *feed me the knowledge.*

"Side mirrors," she starts. "Adjustments/settings. What's the general policy," she asks, "on adjustments?"

"Adjustments can never be by hand, only with electronic relay," he goes on. Hadley nods as he recites, but when she stops, he says "Hello?" or "*Yes?*"

She starts again, maneuvering, teasing, keeping a steady pace.

"Coordination with rearview?"

"*What?*"

Then after a few seconds he says, "That is *not* in there!"

"You're right," Hadley smiles. She wants his mouth turned upwards like a pattern over hers, two gestures of a single face, but she sees how hard it will be to get him out of his tunnel. He is consumed with the studying, knowing it has to be done and waiting to blame Hadley for mistakes, for his having to do it at all, for not being able to download it into himself like a zip disc.

"Fueling." she says. "Static electricity."

"No cell phones," he says. "iPods."

Hadley nods. The book's diagrams have smiley-faced men with white jackets and caps, their raised arms bent at perfect right angles. She read in the paper today of interrogation manuals at Guantanamo that had similar little pictures. *The Army*, she thinks. And then: *the war; it's what I left out.* Of job sources, the list of places that would take out, rescue young guys from this Valley. Those only places, those few.

"Correct," she turns the page. "Police stops," she says, and when he sees there is no room in her face for joking now and there is support in her look, he breathes deep and looks down at the booklet cover.

"Pull over before any fuzzer or siren, on a high berm if you have to."

Hadley nods.

"Hands on wheel, two and ten o'clock. Don't get out."

Jed freezes. They've come to the unthinkable, the must-not-happen, the under-no-circumstances shit sandwich. He is fingering the buttons on his flannel shirt, the ones whose brown and olive blended color matches the checks of the shirt's pattern. She sees he can't go on, but he will.

"If you're asked what you're carrying, hand them the lading bill. Look like you don't know what it's about. The Mexican shrug. Handle it by the edges and shrug your shoulders."

He's winging this, because how could it be in the book? He's running through the scene that's unlikely, that could be pretty close to impossible. The trucks are kept clean and free of anything suspicious, only his driving would get him stopped. But it's the scene that could send him away, if not forever, then at least for the rest of what could be called his youth.

He is thinking, Hadley knows, *Run. If it's one cop, one chippie, then get off into the weeds on the hillside.* He knows how quick he is, a .400 meter man in middle school. And if it's in the alleys and flats of these towns, or someplace in the city, there are places to run behind, little crevices to dart into like scared fish do.

What he's seeing, Hadley thinks, is prison. He seems himself gathering his stuff at the warden's office in middle age, pale and thin, but flabby, skin like the uneven white and translucent muck of a birthday candle. The best of his life behind him, all of it nearly. Nothing but his father's back porch, the old man's stairs and rain-bowed doors. They hear Jed's father now, up in the larder, straightening things, switching off the lights and heading up to the next floor to sleep.

Jed's eyes are squeezed shut, wincing, with tired skin around them like a turtle's.

     RICHARD WIRICK

Hadley shuts the book and moves over to the stereo, plugs in the pod, and starts playing "Band of Gypsies." It's the first record they ever made love to, and the first song, "Freedom," has a tasty backward whip and bridge that takes her breath away.

She moves over to Jed as the guitars skip over themselves, high, chilly, overlapping sheets like those water wall fountains at the mall, solid and steady, but still invisible. He lights a joint and smiles. This is the soft Jed, the calm and welcoming one, the undriven.

He folds Hadley around him, one waterfall sliding into another, as the sweet smoke goes up in the heating air. The mixture of the music and the hooch and the knotty, tenty Mongol curtain of his hair over her as his face starts to strain makes her think of their lives as something larger than this time and place, but still so completely part of it—lives that have risen up in these high, high moments to belong, somehow, to the world.

He is outside his pants now and arched over her, the rope of his hair slapping his forehead. They themselves, they specifically, will never be remembered. But they are lovers of their time, lovers of their time and age and place, who will somehow give it its name.

15.

Right when Hadley was getting ready to ride with Jed the first time, Mrs. McNaul died. It was all over the papers. Her husband had moved out of the house with their two girls and was living with them in a cabin up in Arrowhead. Supposedly she was trying to really, finally get clean. Mr. McNaul had given her an ultimatum, but ultimatums to somebody who's been using that long are useless things, the strongest words having no more force than the weakest ones. They exchange the language they are expected to, but really the sounds are nothing, pieces of trash, like smashed cans or something. They kick them down the chasm they stand at together, watching them fall away into the emptiness.

Mrs. McNaul—Cassie was her first name—had started going out with a younger guy who worked in a rest home. He was a decade her junior, but looked even more decimated than she did. Crank had gotten more powerful in the shorter number of years he had been using it. Its octane rose in multiples. Its power was deceptive. Hadley thought of the falls at Yosemite, how it was like that. It cooled you with its mist. It welcomed you. But there were walls and walls of power behind what you saw, waiting to chop and scatter you.

The two of them had driven up toward Big Bear, some think to find the girls, get close to them and talk and let them get to know Pradeep. He was Sri Lankan, a tall, beautiful man and a sort of nurse. But they got lost.

What probably happened is they started shooting as they left the City, and got disoriented and turned off the 10 onto a low desert county road that wound back through the San Jacinto foothills.

They were very high even when they made the first calls for help, because they made no sense and weren't able to guide the sheriff's dispatcher. Their voices were weak, little pleas. They talked to each other about blankets and water as much as they talked to the rescuers, and the tapes played on the news showed that in those moments they had really forgotten they were on the phone. They were like children who had dropped it and were pushing the wrong buttons in their confusion.

They pulled in helicopters from eastern counties to help look, searching the high, cold roads—cold even in summer—that had only letters or numbers, like the trails on Hadley's drumlin maps.

A calf was bleating in the dark when the searchlight found the big mound of sand that covered their car. The calf was caught in barbed wire, but had pulled its bloody neck loose and stood there with its saucer eyes shooting back the flashlight beams.

They were frozen to death inside the car, curled up under a sleeping bag with their foreheads stuck together by frost crystals. On their cellphones were messages from a deputy telling them they'd been spotted and to stay put. There were two other voicemails, angry ones from the husband telling them to go away.

Those cries, the little voices. They played them over and over on Channel 4 with shots of the sleeping bag and video of the gurneys going into the EMT vans. At the end there weren't even words, only sounds, words falling back into sounds on their way to silence. It made Hadley think of Vincent Price in "The Fly," the horrible, fantastic head sticking out of the hairy sheen of the little insect body in the web. *Help me.*

The stations played them so much, Hadley thinks, because there was more than sadness and warning in the voices. The voices seemed closer to love than anything else. Love stripped down to a final, pure longing, with everything, every last thing, cut away from it. It reminded her that the most desperate lovers were the most pure, those calling in from lost places and hanging from only their own energy, like acrobats who'd dropped the pole and were clutching the wire until it cut them.

The love of those out at the edges, the margins. It was the most bright and pitiful. It was, to use a Blake word, the most "baleful." It was the most black.

At the funeral Hadley's mother is following her like a dog, sniffing into her shawl, watching for whatever she can pick up in the way Hadley looks at the others. Trying to see with whom her daughter is most familiar. Seeing if Hadley is somebody dangerous enough, close enough to it, to be able to satisfy all of her nosy hunger. The way she hangs on Hadley is worse even than the Stare. It is like the Stare in motion, the walking and talking version of the Ray.

But there is nothing in Hadley's face in the way of information. For a few nervous seconds Hadley wants to make a face at her mother, something hideous and inappropriate. But she just walks closer to Jed, to his scornful Daddy. She'd rather have his whip, his cold steel, than her mother's flapping suction cup, her surprise hypnotisms.

Hadley finds it strange to stand in the light of day, in the way it picks up all the stones and clods of the pile the diggers made and the uneven colors of canvas under the casket on its roller, the elevator that takes it down below the awful ground they walk on. It is all so bright and detailed here where it rubs against what it's not, its opposite—the end of the human, down there where the pulley stops and the long, long nothing starts.

II

16.

Jed and Hadley are in the cab of his truck going down 395 toward the city, and they've just come to the I-5 interchange. This is where everything slows, and the drivers start to simmer in their little cases of hot glass and tin, even with the AC on or both windows down for a cross-breeze if the AC's busted. Dust rises above the river of cars. The haze made by the hot, hard ground and car exhaust is the last thing anybody wants—the last reason anybody would enter a free-way—but it is really the first and only thing you can count on in this city. Getting on. And somehow, eventually, getting off.

The horns start, like an orchestra tuning. If hell had a sound, this would be it. Indian and Sri Lankan drivers in panel trucks like theirs wave their bare arms outside the windows like bent crabs' feet that move faster the more the texture and the pressure of the air begins to cook them. Most of the trucks have Spanish lettering: Morales y Fils; Matamoros and Puebla; Oaxaca, Oaxaca, Oaxaca, everybody seems to be from Oaxaca or Oaxaca State. A lot of the Central Americans are in tiny pick-ups crowded with men and leaf-covered equip-ment. The *pachecos* are young and strong and browned by the sun, they bounce up and down.

All of China seems to have come to these shores, the newly-landed scrunched down in white vans with fading characters and long racks of hangers swaying inside the back windows. Cambodians and Vietnamese are in gardening trucks also, and lift their feet up from the heating floor-boards, flip-flops loose on their toes. Black people, who used to do the jobs these people do, are rarer now to see but still fly by in plumbing trucks emblazoned with smiling, muscled, Nordic uber-plumbers carrying small grey boxes filled with tubes and joints and pellet-sized water remedies.

And all the Valley people are still here; they've just been over-taken by this multi-colored U.N. assembly of the interstate. Okies and descendents of such places still sidle by in board-sided flatbeds and salesmen's company cars, some of them smoking, drinking, chewing, text messaging and talking on cellphones. Cigars have made a comeback lately, the men chewing off tips and tapping away big clumps of ashes that spray along their windows and fenders like reams of sun-dried, disintegrating birdshit. Most of the Okies are still blue-collar: single-crop farmers and drywall men, carriers of ladders and slathers of balanced tubs of glue and paste, barrel strappers. They have long hair and sideburns under their backwards ballcaps, singing to Lynyrd Skynyrd and Journey riffs and working their sunburned jaws with gobs of snuff.

But types, categories? For all Hadley knows, there are really none of these. A black man is as likely to be driving a Bentley as a Bug. Men with turbans adjust their ties, and a sleek, grey-suited executive woman wears a gauze-white Mennonite hat with dangling lace-up laces, like a surgeon's cap.

The old, plain, predictable America disintegrates like a tumbling, cooking space capsule in this atmosphere of the New Pacific corridor. Skin color and clothes and headwear are festive or somber or loud with no logical relation to who you'd think was wearing them. America used to be a bottle of homogenized milk with cream on top, but now it's a suspension of crushed glass, like the Tiffany lamp Hadley saw suspended from the ceiling of an old Fresno hotel lobby the other week—a thing of active fire, of new, self-making combinations, shining of its own light, waiting, wavering.

The cars go faster now. Jed has to concentrate more. They get to the far north San Fernando Valley with its swales and gorges made of the end moraines Hadley's maps tell her stopped the ice, so the glaciers could drop their stone loads like dump trucks. The woods suddenly end and they see the towns that her father said looked old, but that were built only in the eighties, the decade of money-making, or in the nineties, the decade of baby-making.

These places have no center, no squares with court-houses or churches. The centers of the towns are malls where people congregate, sometimes only to be inside somewhere with AC or to sink their hands wrist-deep in fountains of cold water. A toddler drowned in one of the fountains not long ago, his Gymboree clothes spinning bright as a pinwheel in the foamy ripples.

Fast food, gasoline, Jiffy Lube. It all flies by. A bomber would never know what to hit, each patch the same as the one down the road. The trees here—big now, planted when Hadley was born—shake off the clouds of dust the pebble beds throw up at them all afternoon. In the wake of the cars ahead of them, they pull back toward their path magnetically, jerking, swirling in all directions like something pulled from the invisible into the visible.

By the time they are in the South Valley, what everyone thinks of as the Valley, the Valley-Valley, the cars around Jed and Hadley fill with women in track suits and designer sunglasses, riding up even with them in their SUVs and jabbering on pimped-up, fake jeweled GPS's, or seemingly conversing with just the air until Hadley can see the dark tear-shaped Bluetooth devices clipped on their ears like roaches or one of those terrible, wine-stain birthmarks. *Hemangioma.*

Big dogs ride on the seats of a lot of these cars, standard poodles or afghans, and lean their big dog heads out of programmed safety windows, so their ringletted coats flatten and quiver and their slobber sprays along the side windows like frogs' eggs. Convertibles cruise filled with school kids, girls usually, driving these expensive cars to their private schools in Holmby Hills or Bel-Air, "prep lite," as Hadley's father mockingly calls the places. Jed looks down at the girls' cleavage—they wear those kinds of dresses to these schools—and none of them ever looks up from the radio dial or phone screen full of floating, glowing digits. Their focus is always only on what's in the car, what's in front of their faces. Nothing else exists for them.

* * *

Finally they are at the end of the 5 freeway and merging onto the Glendale, with brown scrub hills like at home sprouting from what's usually much greener, the drought having had that effect. The zoo and the Gene Autry Museum straddle the highway, but most of the buildings are still just warehouses and Armenian machine shops, with people walking the thirsty streets like thin, wobbly shadows in the heat. The names on the building's sides all end in "ian" and are stacked in the middle with "Vs" and "Ks" that flake away along the dry facades, looking like blemishes on a rose.

Suddenly, from around the headlands and the Pasadena hills, the skyline appears. The hazy brown outskirts and old, "close-in" neighborhoods look mulchy and rotten and bumpy as they run on into the higher, ripened stacks of new executive apartments and skyscrapers. All of them here, built mostly in the eighties, look for some reason like wedding cakes covered with coconut icing, and little iron elbows tapering over lower stories like upside down coat hooks. Hadley can see the bright little confetti of hotel flags along Figueroa and Flower streets before the traffic slows again, pulling them toward the final, shade-chilled tunnel of Chavez Ravine.

RICHARD WIRICK

17.

Hadley knows they are in the flower district, she just doesn't know where. Jed is driving the truck like he knows where he's going, but he hasn't been in this section of the city any more than she has, which is not at all. Big flower carts block the streets until Hadley sees one very odd and flat one. She realizes it's a garment dolly—the flower and garment districts converge in these barrios around the PG&E complex. The street signs are in Spanish, the stall markers in Tagalog. Forklifts back out of garage doors right into the street and whirl around like wide-jawed, angry beetles.

Jed keeps driving, not reacting to anything until they turn onto San Pedro Street, and Hadley remembers this is also Skid Row, the first and only one, the Place Itself. Crowds of ghost-white men of all colors stand in the street, swaying and scratching themselves, animals in a meadow sleeping standing up.

Jed has to steer clear of the men, and he spins the wheel, the truck jerking violently. The street seems too small for a truck of this size, or maybe it's the conflagration of people on it, and they have a hard time dodging men running out from fenced lots with their arms extended and women peeing down out of of their skirts onto flat, oily stands of cardboard.

They get off the street but the men are sprinkled down onto East Eighth, the big boulevard of the plant and posie business. They stand out by the parking meters with contraptions that slip a coin down into the slots, which they do for people willing to give the real coins to them. Some have problems with it; they pull at the wires or bang the head of the meter; the parkers, mostly shy, composed white people, stand by nervously, shrugging off their complicity. Some of the shoppers give up or wave their hands. Others run when the parking men pull the real coins out of their pockets to give back to them.

Hadley leaves the Mapquest printout on her bent knees now, giving directions and adjusting the window height. Jed gives a grimace to every street, especially every small street, she tells him to turn down, as if he isn't convinced or feels it is a route he knows and detests. Hadley is not convinced either, but Darko the Serbian, whose drop this will be, dictated the directions to Natasha's brother two nights ago.

They see Darko's people in the narrow places they turn down now. The shadows of the buildings make the small streets dank and clammy, a place where some kind of eternal evening is stored. Men have been run out of here by the cops, their shopping carts left behind filled with piles of blankets and bags of other bags, and papers and laundry shirt-boards and flattened cans.

At the end of the final street, in a shaft of light, they see the large shadow of Darko waving his arm in the sunlight. They hadn't been getting a signal from the phone number they'd been punching in, so Hadley wonders if he knew to be out here from his famous sixth sense, or maybe just timed them. As they slow down in front of the building, Darko and another guy slowly push the barn-sized garage door open, and in a minute they are in.

Jed leans out of the window and clasps Darko's hand like they are long lost buddies. Darko helps him down. Hadley gets out her side—"Yugos don't help women," Nat had told her—and walks around and shakes the hand of the Basin's ephedra god. He wears a small black watch cap and has a couple of gold teeth and one silver tooth in front. What is amazing is his pores, how big they are and how black their filled holes look. He's been lifting, and even in the cool of the building his skin glistens.

He laughs and shoos Hadley away, knowing from Jed's early call that she wanted to be away from all this as it was happening. She's agreed with Jed to be picked up at a café on the corner, a Mexican liquado place.

When she leaves, she looks back to wave and sees the automatics stuck down the pants of Darko and all his men.

　　　　　　　　　　　　　RICHARD WIRICK

18.

Hadley's older writing instructors tell her never to read just before she writes, but she brought some Milton to knock off in the café before going back into the essay on the tortoise. And the Milton is not even *Areopagitica* or *Apology for Poetry*; it's something on divorce and why the Catholic regime should allow it, and it flows and turns and unhinges, snaps shut again, and like the chilliest breeze blows open new doors and windows in her head.

JC, the much younger writing instructor, who they all call Tim, has strict guidelines that she pretty much stays inside. He doesn't want any TV or video or fashion references, what he calls electric malarkey, and is most comfortable with what he dubs the pre-cyber aesthetic—one that restores prose to the state it occupied before its videographic dissipation. It's in keeping with his conservative bearing and values. Hadley's friends can't imagine a writer who looks like something out of West Point or the young Mormon Elders at Brigham Young. But he does. In fact, Tim is *in* the military. He's in the Reserves and, if Iraq keeps up, may end up packing his journals with his boots and pistol and driving down to Pendleton in the middle of the night, flying off to the suck in the belly of a C5-A (the plane Hadley's father *almost* designed).

Hadley sets the tortoise out on its dusty path. Berries and insects draw him through his sweet umber sea of dust. *The cells that make up the eyes replenish first, in this most cell-replacing of creatures. How else but through furious, almost undirected cell change, cell change bordering on malignancy, could an organism routinely live twelve or fourteen decades?*

Too scientific: Break it down and kindle some fire around it. *The cells of the eyes are replenished twice a year. This is a creature of peren-*

nially unstable cytology, giving him completely replenished life with each cycle, so the years stretch out and wait for him, pulling him forward, handing him longevity as it is given to no other earthly creature.

Out the window are the local fabric merchants' kids, skateboarding, zipping their figure-eights around the drunks and pie-crust flower pots into the dumpster. Rows of dark blue tattoos go down their arms. A solid row of ink like this is called a "sleeve." Their belts hang heavy with electriviata. Hadley watches their hips sway off in the shade of San Julian Street, the devices on their waists blinking red and orange in the leaves.

The same with the café manager. He wants to walk around while he talks on the phone, so he has a pimped-up cordless that looks as big as the first cell phones, before they started slimming down. Nobody wants to be held down in the process of connection. The idea of communicating from a table, a fixed point, is gone. All this cyber maneuverability lets us be everywhere at the same time, but never very deeply, always less than completely. Being everywhere, but being on a sheet of glass laid over things and never touching them… so the years stretch out and wait for him. When Hadley writes that, she's in the moving animal. She's inside the feel of time's long emptiness. She's not outside of anything: the grains of soot and gravel live in the letters as she's making them.

Forward, forward, past any other earthly creature. The manager looks at her strangely. This isn't a café.

A plank slams into the dumpster's side. The kids are playing a game they learned online but playing it for real, down here in life. It's like when Hadley first put on good earphones; the Smiths' song making what I saw into a video for itself, the bell-stream of Jonny Marr's guitar giving everything a glad new grace.

She goes another good two paragraphs. The tortoise uses the shade of his shell to soak his skin and insides, however hot it is. The tortoise is utterly unconnected, as free of his surrounding vessel as a hermit crab. But he keeps it. He never leaves. And thus his timelessness. It's like the bark of a Sequoia.

She thinks of the instant messaging Jed was doing with Darko's warehousemen on the way down here. No more a kind of talking than the avoidance of talk, the shorthand of phrases and mini-formulas they do with one another face-to-face. Almost not able to wait for it to end.

Jed will be calling any second. He should be finishing about now. The more Hadley writes, the less hungry she is, the more she refills her coffee. To the café manager, she is an unproductive customer. *A margin customer.* The skateboard kids are Hungry Chucks, talking pod to pod in a fast-moving sweat. When they're done they are as hungry as someone who's just worked out.

Tim is right. About the electric malarkey. Maybe we're at our peak right now as a species, Hadley thinks, with all these zaps and blinks and screens talking up at us out of our flabbergasted hands, into our ears from dark teardrops. It's like the mountains around their Valley. Each has a heart, a secret place, a cave or stream or grove of trees that is its heart. It could be the summit, but usually it's not. Cyber's the summit but not the heart. Cyber's the highest we've gone, and damn impressive at that. But it's not the heart. It's not the Thing Itself. It ain't the main machine.

What *is* is what she's scratching out now: descriptions of a round brown slowly plodding plate of ancient newness, with the words she uses to tell of him flaking and falling off and blowing over his leathery neck and waxy cracking toes, his eyeballs with their irises split into fine root hairs of blood, tiny rivers of crimson lines.

She takes the phrases and turns them around. She picks them up and turns them around again. And then again she turns them around. The words are like skaters doing figure eights, deepening into their form as a body, the sureness returning and replenishing itself, growing.

Her cell rings as the manager brings the meager check, the tiny two-line charge. It's Jed's number that lights up and pulses. She's got the feel of the tortoise now. His completeness is also Hadley's, for now. For now, his perfection is her perfection. She shuts her pad and reaches for the phone.

19.

Hadley's feet are up on the dash on the slow ride home, rush hour stuffing back everything going toward the valleys and the northeast. She could tell there was something in Jed's face when he pulled over at the curb in front of the café and leaned over to pull up the door lock, and she climbed up the high, high step into the cab.

Jed is talking about the traffic, the heat, the landscape of Burbank and Glendale. He points to the curved, copper-colored backs of the WB studios and says that's where the MGM musicals were made.

"Jed."

He pulls down the sun visor, looks over at Hadley too quickly to catch her eye. Then his eyes are back on the road and the setting, still-hot sun.

"What *happened* in there?" Hadley asks.

"What happened is that the cut is good on the runs. But I'd be driving all the time."

"But everybody works *all the time.* That's *what work is.*"

Jed pulls on his sunglasses, which have dropped down from the visor.

"Even them," Hadley says, pointing over the edge of the freeway to the studio roofs.

"There are economies…" he starts.

She's looked back out the window.

"Can I finish?" he asks.

She sighs and stares straight ahead.

"There are economies of scale. You can't keep putting your labor in, unit by unit, and getting back a salary, unit by unit."

Men appear again on roofs, or ladders on the curved roofs. The ladders are curved also, the men's shadows flattening.

　　　　　　　　　　　RICHARD WIRICK

"You need," Jed says, "to make a leap. There has to be a point where return makes a jump. A qualitative leap. To reward imagination. The mind-fuel you've put in."

Hadley thinks she is recognizing this from an *Utne Reader* story she saw a week ago on Darko's table. It lay open where Jed was reading it, and it had tables and steps and scales climbing skyward.

"That's why you study. That's why you get something real going."

"Like you? Like JC and writing class?"

This stings, a place he's never gone before. However long they've known each other, whoever was on the floor never pulled at the other one, never pulled them down. Jed knows this takes the wind out of Hadley, knows how long it could leave her silent.

"*Now* is what I need, Hadley. Now. Now. Now. Those three words."

"I know now. I know now. Do you know what somebody in prison knows about 'now'?"

He slams the wheel, dust coming up out of the seams of the fabric. "Other people can do this. This piecemeal stuff."

Crocuses are coming out in the hills around Eagle Rock, bright yellow, nested in what look like little praying hands of green. Their thousands of drooping snowdrop heads have rivered together and pulse up under the haze like inverted lightning forks. What is wildest seems somehow to have the most pattern: this fire from the ground an errorless accident, an undirected diagrammatic grid, something deep down in the dirt but looking to Hadley like the flow of the supernatural.

"You and I don't get ahead like this, me working for a dollar a day. We'll never be able to move forward."

The "You and I" gives Hadley's heart a flip, a teeter-tottering at first and then a blowing open like a flimsy door. The "We'll" is nice too. She isolates it from the "never" and lets it pulse and rise, lets it shine out of the dead matter of the other words. He's never talked of the two of them like this, in a future time. He's never said anything like "going forward."

"I should have guys doing this for *me*," he says. "Charging Darko flat for each delivery and paying them, like minimum wage."

"But then you're further in. You're management already. "

"Maybe not," he says, looking toward Hadley, because he knows he's being convincing when that happens. She won't look back, she won't validate. "I may *not* be management. I don't know *what* I am. I mean, I'm all the more out of it by not driving THIS thing. And with what I'm going to describe, everything's cash, and nobody talks. I'm only connected to transactions, not to things."

Hadley balances her crazy happiness with the dread of her knowledge that this is something new, something completely separate from delivery, transport. He senses her sense of a new and barely knowable thing, a brand new branch of the trail.

"What is it?" She tries to make her voice uninterested, but welcoming whatever he has.

But he won't tell her now that they're moving more quickly, shaking off trucks and limos and exiting, blinking older drivers, seeing how fast the truck can really go.

And for this moment, Hadley really *doesn't care*, nestling over into him, his big blue jean-jacketed arm clamping around her like the guard on a carnival ride. *You and I.* There was a song on one of her father's records that had that line as a chorus. By Country something. Country Bob or Country Jim, one of the old hippie bands. Written by somebody famous to his other famous lady fair, the two of them flying across the desert between what they knew were great darknesses, singing and singing, following only the singing.

20.

The new thing, the better thing, Hadley finds out, is one of those uniquely crank things. Since users have a lot of time on their hands, they borrow their money-making schemes—their "economies of scale," as Jed would have it—from daytime layabout burglars or "Min-Sec" rookies. And one of the commonest ways to get up cash, and to hardly ever get caught, is check washing.

It's what Jed has been getting at on the drive, something Hadley had already read a lot about in the papers. Where goeth crank, goeth the newest and most unique of crime waves. And the newest physical plant and paraphernalia.

Check washing is beyond counterfeiting, beyond forgery, beyond anything the world of paper money transactions ever contemplated, The check washer breaks into a mailbox, preferably a rural mailbox, one of the stand-alone jobs you see craning their stilt-bird necks out to the government's daily emissary, red flag up, something to take. And it won't just be the box of an obscure country clod, but one that belongs to a home-run small business or a country squire plopping healthy coin into an annuity.

The washer brings his handful of envelopes to a soaking tray, opens them, and after putting special tape on the signature that makes it good, begins the process of letting the water—the universal solvent—do its work.

If the checks are written by hand and not typed, all their writing will rise, slowly, ghostlike, from the paper up into the tugging liquid. Though she's never seen it, some say the script will hover whole for awhile before dispersing, so that someone looking down sees the disembodied writing and behind it a shadow of itself on the space where it was first set down, a primitive holograph. Empty of all but executed signatures, the checks are dried on clothesline until payees of the washer's choice are entered, people whose IDs the washers have stolen or cribbed or outright created: cobbled together from online virtuality.

Check-washing has usually been the province of users, people too strung out and zapped and horny to hold down jobs, and who use it as their sole income. But Darko got the idea of splitting up the troops of people driving cross-country to get over-the-counter phedra and using them to rob mailboxes, as phedra supplies were coming now from regular sources: truck hijackings by Pimo Indian gangsters, cargo thieves who had been boosting rigs for years on the inland roads.

So mothers sat out at clusters of mailboxes—actually *down the road* from these treasure ships—in their cars with newspapers, children, Styrofoam cups and pets and those silver windshield sun deflectors, and waited for that window between flag-up and drive-up by the mailman in his three-wheeled moon module. Usually the women struck just as the people got back in their houses, when there was little chance they would turn around and reflect on the their negligible task.

"No way in hell," I say to Jed. "It's larceny, plain and simple. Prison stuff, as in felonies. What in *the hell* are you thinking?"

"Same thing as with transport. None of this shit touches me. I'm dispatching the Check Moms and supervi—well, *looking in on* the washers."

"Looking in on. You can't tell me there's no record of this, no way of tracking you."

He puts his full, open hands together like the praying nuns in old paintings, brings his fingertips to his nose.

"Darko says I don't even need to use my *name*. I'll use another name."

"I'm sorry," Hadley says, though she knows he's not paying attention. "But this is dirty. It will make you dirty. It will stick to you like glue."

He won't open his eyes or take his hands away from his nose.

"You're dirty," Hadley says. And superimposed over all this, almost as if it were a film on a pulled-down screen between the two of them, is the image of him really going down: standing at an arraignment, in a jumpsuit, shackled. Being driven away from his conviction in a van, the last freedom he'll ever know. Her heart going away with all of it, locked in the dented panel and exhaust smoke of the marshal's transport.

"Look," she says, "I trust you. But right now I don't know if you're thinking clearly. You're too hungry. You're reaching in too far."

He begs indulgence with that catching his lip on his tooth, pulling back a strip of his hair that makes his forehead so gorgeous. But she's looking into him, right down to the bottom. He's taking her stare full-bore, like a frozen, stinging gas he has to inhale as part of some unpleasant medical procedure.

"It's either this, or I need to move. Move on."

Hadley won't look at him with this old trump of his, and she rolls her eyes. This card is always his last.

"Fine," she says.

"Hadley," he says.

"Go," she says.

He looks at her. Now he's spitting the gas back at her, the icy liquid, the hideous freeze. It is like that because she never knows what it will do to her seconds or minutes later. She knows it will have an effect, she just doesn't know what. It's a standoff, the worst kind.

"Come and see," he says. "It's all I ask. The one thing I ask."

"I'm *afraid*. We might get taped just walking into a washing room."

"We'll wear glasses, and you know, I don't know if I'll ever even have to be there. To be in one."

"You can…."

"I can work by phone, by pay-card phones. Throwaways."

She *has* gone along with him on other jobs, and feels the pleasure of tolerance pushing her, rolling up out of her interlocked heart and eyes. But she draws the line here or she'll never draw it. She'll never make the point.

They stand there like tired boxers, and, like tired, battered men in the ring, they fall into one another's embrace, still tugging, still

ready to hit, to fake, to see the other unbalanced and helpless.
The warmth of him washes over her, softening.

"You go," she says. "And come back and tell me about it."

RICHARD WIRICK

21.

There are compartments in the head. Like those closet organizers, or the tiny Chinese lacquer box drawers she sees in giant cabinets they sell at Pier 1, stained brown, made to look a hundred years old. It might have been Fitzgerald who said you were a genius to carry contradictory notions around without breaking down, without being forced to choose between them.

But really it's just the way most people live their lives: one thought here, another, glaringly different, one there. Intending something at one moment and then a truly opposite thing the next. Not just slightly different, but opposite. Truly, unbelievably opposite. We may be rational, but that has never, ever meant consistent. It's like the earthquakes. You're in one, you're dying of fright, you roll around. You won't go in underground parking for months.

But you don't move. You don't even let yourself think of it. The practical solution dissolves as soon as it comes into your mind. You stay. You're jumpy. You start to feel quakes and temblors that aren't even there.

But you don't leave. In fact, if you can, you go and buy a house.

* * *

Hadley looks like Jackie O. coming in here: dark turtleneck, straw hat, oversized sunglasses, pants rattling in the wind, walking down a New York street like a lonely, lovely scarecrow. And she feels like that, particularly fragile, lonesome, skinny, scurrying along the margins. Up behind everything, watching on a stool. Behind the partitions, silently observing. Like she is now.

It seems to be the same place they were cooking that one day, or part of the same complex: low roof, shadowy and dank, but with open doors and a cross-breeze that blows the day's heat off and keeps it away. Lamps on the tables and mainly girls in Indian print blouses, leaning over and watching the checks go in the water, and the water doing its work. Some of them stand for five, ten minutes, not moving their heads.

Maybe they see something fascinating there. Hadley remembers a groundhog her father had hit with the car, how he'd thrown it in a rain barrel under the shed at the lot where he finally built their house after clearing its stand of trees. They animal floated in the water for months, and for a long time, when Hadley lifted the lid, it was just the same as it had been when it was dead on the road—brown, inert, its white teeth bared and its clutched paws drifting at the barrel bottom only a little less stiffly than if it had been out in the air. But after a few months the form of the thing floated up as purely white as a ghost to the water's top. And there was a numinous trail winding from the carcass to the floating apparition, like a tunnel or a tornado's column, a sort of birth canal, pushing the flesh and fur up to its filmy afterlife.

From her perch, Hadley imagines the check inks to be this way. She's assuming they float intact, in different colors and in their assorted rolling-tip or ballpoint textures, up on the flat surface of the pans as clearly as the reflections of lights and ceiling tiles that waver there.

The girls leaning over them are all younger than Hadley. Where are their mothers? They must only do the driving, the box-pinching. They are the older cadres, and these are the yeomen. There is something criminal but something incredibly, sufferingly innocent in the way the girls bend over their work. They are solemn as they lift the checks out, but once in awhile they will talk to one another, and great screeches of seagull laughter will go up.

Jed is miles away, making another delivery to the North Valley, and Hadley has promised in good faith to stay here until their shift ends, she, who vowed on her life, never to come. She has one of her geo service maps with her, of moraines and slurries that formed Sand Canyon, a place with gullies so deep that Aerojet used it to bury

　　　　　　　　　　　　RICHARD WIRICK

rocket fuel waste here for decades. These maps are smaller than the others, in a hard, laminated format like the freeway maps they sell at Stop-n-Go.

Hadley remembers that Darko is coming in for some kind of inspection, at which time she wants to be long gone, away from here.

The Sand Canyon moraines are thick with rubble from the glaciers: boulders that show up as siena-colored ovals and slightly darker circles within circles, signifying broken stone masses whose high tops have pushed up slowly through ten thousand years of soil layers. Buttes rise up in pairs and threes like squarish railroad cars, backing through the same soil layers from the same tectonics, the same plate movement, as if a god were pushing his fist through piles of stacked, tottering dishes. The subtler markings are even thicker here than on full-sized charts, the screens and scrims of tiny crosses and houndstooth commas swarming like gnats over fruit, signifying precipitation, water courses and bodies of water, aquifers. They are colored purple: lavender and indigo, periwinkle. Dress pattern colors. Looking closer, she sees how easily terrain and elevation signs are hidden down inside them. They are like fly-swarms, patches of smoke that camouflage what's underneath. Hadley stares and stares until the larger shapes bulge up through these smaller wisps and fizzes.

A truck pulls up outside. The girls straighten the fronts of their shirts and touch their hair. When the knock comes they are silent, immobile. All of them look down into the pans.

22.

Darko comes in in his black leather coat, his hair mussed by the wind and his riding goggles stuck up in the middle of them like a nesting bird. The goggles have left a white band around his eyes like a Lazy 8 or infinity sign, and Hadley remembers this raccoon patch always being there in whatever weather, whatever season, whether he is riding his bike or not. Jed calls this his "reverse ghost" look, which doesn't make sense, though Hadley sees what he's getting at, and which is why she is the writer and not Jed.

Darko puts his jacket on the door peg. He whacks it with his fist to get the dust out. The women jump.

When he is walking along behind them, Hadley sees that the girls are not just bending out of fear, or from watching the checks, but because they are, well, *bent*. Crank plays hell with your calcium. It bats at the body and bends the bones over. It does something where the brittleness that's supposed to come from aging reverses, and things go back to plastic, like with the greenstick fractures of small children.

Darko walks along behind the row of them like a visiting president reviewing an honor guard. He squints and bends down, stirring the water in a pan with his finger. The girl whose tray it is shudders. Her hair is stiff and oblong, like a wind-blown desert bush. Hair is another casualty. For all their wakefulness, users seldom get it under the shower water.

Darko says something—something critical—to the girl, which makes her grimace, her lips peeled back over her teeth. The teeth of these people! At first it's just the smoking that stains them. But then something gets going with the gums, or the bones under the gums, and the bottoms of the teeth start to weaken. The ridges on their tips discolor. Their sides wear away. The enamel comes off like beetle-eaten hickory bark, and then they're open to anything: soft wood, soft pulp, soft tissue craving its return to a vegetable state.

They don't get to dentists until there's nothing left to do but pull the teeth. It became an epidemic out in the middle of the country, and it's given, sadly or not, new wind to the sagging fortunes of dental practices. This girl is well on her way, though still in the staining phase, the faint brown creeping across the white like flower petals tarnishing.

He spots a girl on the opposite side hanging a check, meticulous with the clothespin, and asks her why there's still writing visible on the paper. Before she can answer he is on her, over her, banging the edge of the table with satisfaction at the sureness of his eye.

"There's WRITING there. Compression," he says, pointing.

She wears a hoodie with a Fresno State bulldog on it, ash-stained, slick and shiny with grime.

"I thought it was the best...."

"You could do with ballpoint?" he finishes.

He tips back the hood until it flops on her neck. He doesn't touch her. He peers around.

"Ballpoint. *Ballpoint*. Three or four washes. And sometimes the tip will break an ink layer."

She is huddled, silent.

"How many washes?"

"Three, I think."

"Then four. *Fucking FOUR!*" he says, the first rising of his voice. "Then you can see if the tip has cracked it."

He is holding the corner of the long form, yellow paper, and when she reaches up to it, he holds it tight for a minute, teasing, not giving it up.

Her eyes are sparkling in the foggy bunker air, and he fixes on her like iron moving toward a magnet. More than anything, the sex is what pulls users into one another. It makes them hungry, ravenous, sometimes indiscriminate. *Always* indiscriminate, really. Dopamine spills through the brain and down into the channels and rivers of blood. The flesh engorges. The flesh needs release. The flesh doesn't care who. "Dopa-motive," Jed calls it, and jokes about trying it when

Hadley's been cold to him.

From behind, Darko takes the girl's hand. Her head goes down with empty, unconvincing coyness. He pulls her up by the wrist like someone drawing a swimmer up into a boat. There isn't enough room here, but she whispers something to him, probably about a truck of hers outside. His jacket is on, and when he opens the door, the light shaft makes everybody wince, picking up the girl's bright patches of acne. She scratches her palm, like everyone using. The same spot, the same itch, in the center of the hand.

23.

Jed is in the kitchen with his back to Hadley, the way he is so much of the time now, smoking a cigar with one hand and bringing the other around to hitch up his pants by the loops. Gestures like these are what Hadley has now, like legends on her maps: she looks at them and checks another place for their sense, hoping she's guessing right. There is so little face to face now, almost never him up above her with his hair wet and eyes tight, shouting out.

She'd tell him to turn around, but she knows she wouldn't see any more. There'd be no more in his face than in the fabric of his shirt. It would be the same. The back is the front, the front the back.

She knows Darko passed Jed over for the washing super-gig when Jed started itching a lot. It was his palms at first, but then his chin and neck. He'd draw his finger down along his jaw, and just when it got to the tip, he'd scratch very fast, scratching, scratching faster, moving back up toward the ear. He had a way of swinging his head from side to side, as if his hand were still and the movement of his head was doing the scratching.

"Darko is Bluebeard. Hefner, something."

The ash of the cigar is an inch and a half long. He told Hadley once not to knock it because a long ash cooled the draw of the smoke. Veterans held the cigar straight up and let it go two, three inches before it fell away.

"He's a creep. He crawled on some girl at the bunker and took her away."

"What makes him that way is what makes him effec—" Jed coughs, his hand dipping, the smoke streaming out.

"What makes him that way is the skunk, Jed."

He turns around now and Hadley sees she is right.

"What makes him that way is what makes him a nod," Jed looks at the ash pile, a little star on his boot.

"And you're defending him. Jesus. He wouldn't cross the street for you. He wouldn't cross the street to shit on your face."

"Hadley, he's hustling. He needs R & R. The man has his hobbies."

"His hobbies? His *hobbies*? That's something you'd say if you'd grown up in the Eighties. He's a vulture. A zombie. He'll throw you away."

"He's the only one I *know* Hadley. *Knowing*, remember? We decided that was most of it, whatever you ended up doing. Whose pocket you could get into."

"Each time it's something new. Same old direction but with brand new horseshit. Each time you get nowhere."

"Darko's thinking of something. He's onto new stuff. If the wash house is so bad, why would you want me there?"

"What I want is for you to get some traction, get *going*. To stop thinking this kind of shit's real."

He puts his other boot on top of the grey pile. He kicks it, spreading the sand-fine, inverted cone of tobacco around the floor.

"It's the beginning of something, a horse I can really ride now. You know me. You know it's a rung on a ladder. A real ladder."

He's looking straight at her. She is shaking her head. Through the blur of the wet in her eyes, he looks sweet.

"I'll take another shift, a night shift he'll give me. They wash the checks by lantern light and use blow dryers to dry."

"I thought he passed you over."

"Passed me over? He *needs* me. The places I know. The people. The markets. The directions. The *things*."

This footing, somehow, has taken Hadley off guard. It was something she thought he'd lost, lost the ability to do, and would concede as much. But now it was like earlier times, when she could talk and talk to him and her words would roll up against nothing, and still she would surge for him.

This is what they have come to. His saving *this* job. She is stopping on a dime and letting him do it. Believe the ladder spiel.

But is it really Hadley that hears him, or some separate thing she has out there just to deflect, absorb? Just to soak up the flack like some kind of decoy? It's the splitting, the splitting away again. She doesn't have the ears or the heart for it anymore. The thing that's listening to him now is the dead twin lying next to the living one. It still sucks as she draws what's left of its blood up through the glassy tube. But she is separate. She turns toward the light. She whitens and goes pink, reaching away.

24.

Hadley's father leans back against his G5 Mac like it is a car fender or a ceiling column in a garage. He's smiling.

"E-mail and evangelism are bad, bad bedfellows," he says.

He runs his pinkie along a column of pdfs from a fundamentalist cousin of his, who lives up-Valley.

"Whatever server failures you see, whatever doom worms are loosed, these guys sail through it all. They have more computing power than anybody, including the Defense Department."

Where was religion in her father's life? Was there any? His mother still crossed the street in Ohio to the Congregational Church her ancestors had built, but he grew up in the Sixties, when religion flew out of people's lives like a trapped bird through an attic dormer. He sympathized with belief. He indulged it as part of his general sympathy for humanity. But Hadley wonders what he would do sitting on the surgeon's couch soaking up the bad news, looking at the terrible X-ray. What would he reach for?

"Wilma here says we ought to support this war, and that something will soon occur to turn the Afghans and Iraqis to Christianity."

"Get out."

"Nope. It's right here. A sort of Paul figure rising up, a mullah who will see the error of his ways and go forth from Monateh, the Mount of the Leopards, and lead the people to Christ."

He makes the Bozo the Clown face he used to make when imitating the children's TV hosts. His eyes blink faster and faster as he widens them, and widens his face and tries to make a surprised "O" with his mouth.

"That guy, I mean the Mullah-Paul, would last about…five minutes?"

RICHARD WIRICK

"Maybe four," he says, squinting at the screen.

After a minute he sighs, still looking at the screen and says, "Yeah."

Talking about Iraq makes them both think of Timmy.

"Sure hope you don't lose your editing partner soon."

Hadley wonders where he's going with this, and just says, "Can you *believe*?"

"Yeah, yeah, I *can* believe. Belief is what does it. Puts new guns in people's hands every day."

"Timmy has a lot here, I mean a lot. He's got school. He's got us."

"Well it ain't enough," he says, scrolling down. "There's something there that's pulling at him, something in that goddamn broken pottery shop."

"I wish I had it. I don't. I want it. I guess I have it when I write, or when I'm trying to write. Or something like it."

"Yeah, that's good. But there's faith and there's Faith," his voice rising like flute notes on the last two words.

He turns the monitor toward Hadley. The picture on it is of a standing woman martyr in flames, her face still beautiful, chains as dainty and contained as bracelets. It was the picture he'd seen on the back of his vinyl copy of the first Leonard Cohen album.

He does this sometimes. Googles something up to put some punch into what he is talking about.

"The one with the *big* F? It makes you give up everything, give up the world. It makes you abandon yourself to the universe. And baby-" he clicks the function icon and scrolls down to the shut-off bar—"you only abandon yourself to the universe when you've got nothing else to lose."

He's said this to Hadley before. It's from some Eliot essay. And, again, she likes him like this, his hair flopped down, loose and coppery, out of a burning brain, throwing off little sparks of insight. Strong in a hidden way, in reserve, in a way Hadley's mother can never be, a way she mocks.

As the screen goes to black he looks straight at Hadley before the dark takes his face.

"You should take over there at the journal. Carry it on for him, until he gets back."

25.

It is just as things start falling into place with Tim, with him leaving and the slot being there for Hadley, with her very own teacher going to Hell Itself so that her chance could come—it is just with these things going right and her up in the air that the other side of the teeter-totter slams down and Jed starts his slide backward, his newest slip in a slipping-down life.

He looks at her less when he talks, looks away like a lying prisoner. He is busier than usual, or makes sure he's looking busy, his collar turned up and his chin darting back and forth in the darkened funnel the fabric makes around his head. His hair is all spikes and nervous squiggles, every look, every thought, little fish flickering away in all that dark Devil's water.

When the faculty advisor, Owen, tells Hadley he wants her to meet with Tim, he takes her first over to a bin where all the submissions are stuffed in manila folders, the folders themselves sticking up end-ways in red welds. She guesses the idea is to have her in control, with her hands on things, when she's first talking to Tim, so he feels the journal, his baby, is "entrusted," "stewarded forward"—Owen's words—while he goes Into the Suck.

Hadley has already looked at some of the stories they've gotten. Some are from here and some from bigger places, the UC schools, Stanford, U. of Washington. Tim once called a group of them Guignol's band, after some blasted-up fragment of tales by Celine. "A parade of awfulness and drek," he went on. Hadley? The few things she's seen, she's generous about: she knows how hard it is to write a good story.

Jed won't come with her to the first meeting with Tim. He says he has to set up another washing mill. Kids on Darko's payroll now

are raking in the checks in droves, harvesting them from the close-
in suburbs like Agoura and Simi Valley, those strange places full of
the architecture of contentment. But who knows if he's lying?

That may be the essence of love: blinding yourself to whether it's
a lie, to whether you can ever know or know that you know. How can
two ever know the same in their knowing?

And what he says now. What it comes out as, what is there to
know about that? The only certain thing about it is its speed, each
word hooked onto the next like zipper teeth. None of it is really talking. It is monotonous, hollow, but always ending with a lift. Unprac-
ticed and perfect, a well polished pitch.

26.

Jed comes in the morning and starts pulling the chairs away from the table, then pushes the table over on its side and leaves it tipped against the wall. The top of the drape sags from its missing runners and he looks up and makes a mean face at the light it's letting in. The column of it shines down through his head like it is empty, as if his head is a paper lantern. He takes a chair from the wall and gets up on it to bunch the fabric and push it out over the curtain rail. This lets light in from the bottom where it's been pulled up and he yells "Fuck." But he steps down off of the chair as quick as a dancer and leans it up against the gap as if it is a magical cello that might explode into splinters.

"We've got something new going on," he says, moving to the kitchen, clearing away glasses, dishes, putting them in the right sink, clearing all the free space with strange, swift moves Hadley has never seen, like a hotel cleaning lady.

"Darko needs some expansion cash. He's gonna involve some Russians, some Romanian guys he knows."

He looks at Hadley as though she should know what this means. She shakes her head. She has somebody's manuscript page in her hand, and all this has happened since the time she started it.

"A heist."

She keeps her head moving.

"We're not going to be involved. We're not going to even know."

Jed is covered with sweat from his cleaning. A bead of it hangs on his nose, and she thinks of what must be inside it, all of the chemicals inside of its clearness.

"I feel sorry for them, Darko. That they have to do this." Hadley has the manuscript sheet in her hand and she thinks of holding it up, its squareness like one of those shields the cops have in other countries. To guard against what might be coming.

She is squaring the manuscript pages, the big envelopes, putting the cap on her blue pencil. She knows the only thing she can do this time is walk. Walk out, not throw Jed out.

The first guy she sees coming up the drive, she knows—Dun Dun. He is one of the Romanians who lives in North Hollywood with his mother, working an import business. These men are all immense, with missing teeth and hair that hangs in ratted strings. Three others are behind him, and Jed stiffens his back as they all four come in.

When each of them is standing in the kitchen, Jed starts the introductions, like they're all greeting each other in a church vestibule. Ass Man is Dun Dun's cousin. He is from the Tyer region of the Upper Volga, where most villages have a population now of one, the gravedigger. Dun Dun is the newest of the group in America and wears a large, OD cigarette burned trench coat that coughs off clouds when he bumps up against anything.

Jed extends his hand toward Bom Dia, who smiles when Jed says he is Brazilian. His mouth has two or three flecks of stained enamel stuffed down in the rows of metal. Biceps shoot out his T-shirt, enormous, beautiful, firm and golden as the bodies of pythons.

Property of Jesus has a tattoo that says those three words in the folds of his neck. When his chin is down, the tattoo lays bunched up like a fishnet waiting to be rolled out to dry. He is from Ukraine. He has a top-heavy, boxlike build and a page boy haircut. There are bandoliers or shoulder holsters under his OD trench, and they bunch up under the fabric like women's shoulder pads, like little bats' wings.

Ass Man drums his fingers on the counter. Property shifts his toothpick.

Jed: "They are going to do something, something completely separate from us, that requires proprietary information."

It's obvious that Dun Dun and Bom Dia don't understand the phrase. The upper skin on Bom Dia's arm twitches like the cheek of a body in sleep.

"Algorithms. Safe lock algorithms."

"I write," Hadley says. "I don't cipher."

"Cipher you need not," said Jed. Dun Dun and Bom Dia are shaking their heads.

"We've got a way to get into some safes, at night. We've got the combinations. But it's night. They've got to be read. And stuck in some kind of paper that hides them, in case we get pinched. The numbers have got to be buried in something."

Jed has never asked Hadley to be involved in new things, in inventions. Projects are something she's pushed to, something she receives. She is the bucket, the funnel. The tubes that all their indirection runs through.

"Your maps," he says.

At first Hadley can't even piece together what he's talking about. Then she knows it's the term moraines. And she's wondering if Jed thinks they glow, if he thinks there's a phosphorescence in them like fiery laketop plankton or the clustered pinpoint maps on planetarium ceilings.

Ass Man has a scar he rubs on the inside of his left hand. Romania. A youth commission before the Fall of '89. Ceascescu, captured, with his wife, having their say at the kitchen table with the soldiers, and then gunned down in a grainy video in their backyard. A place where movies are made now to avoid the cost of the U.S. guilds.

He's from the land of unlikeliness. *It is only a movie*, Hadley thinks, the chill going up in her again like fog. *It is only a beam of light.*

"The crosses, the symbols," Jed says. "We can put the numbers beside them. A figure up by each one."

Hadley sees the nets and bundles of homeomorphs, their perfect and inverse clean right angles. Little digits *could* rest there, in the crook of each one.

Everybody's face is on hers: the last, most necessary link in the chain.

"Get 'em yourself. At the Geo Survey Office."

"They're here," says Jed with his old-eyed plea. He has a glass of water in his hand and puts it down for emphasis, rests his elbows on the counter.

"You've got them. You bought them with cash. I was with you."

          RICHARD WIRICK

Dun Dun and Property look up at the window.

"They could start on them tonight, today if they had to. You could buy a new set when everything is done."

Hadley turns toward the hall and starts back to her room. The door is propped open with a tube, with two tubes. The other ones, empty, lay around with their caps off.

Out the back, through the screen door, a woman walks away. She is carrying half a dozen rolls in a bag.

27.

All around them, around the cooking sheds, are the berms and little knolls and hillocks of slag. The white slag is almost solid; it's been baked in ovens the size of rooms, over fires Hadley imagines pulse and brighten like crimson rivers of lava. Same as the steel mills: Laughlin, Martin. Brightening, never-ending furnaces. Quadrants of iron and stone stuffed high with turning embers.

Sometimes it is ribboned with pink and grey, sometimes a blue-green vein. Veins bring all things liquid and hard. The food inside of everything. The branches of them now, green, coming into her breasts.

The other kind of slag, man-made, is even lighter and pulls itself up in the wind into high, white piles. It isn't always rocky all through; there can be vegetation around the edges. The rockier it is, the crisper the color—mauve or bright beige or just blinding white, like broad sheets hung up and snapping on a line.

Some of the slag pile edges curl over, solid as rock, so in a rainstorm, or if she needed cover from bullets, she could stand just under the bend of them. In winter, steam rises off of them, like the small round pipes that chug out smoke from the Jed-gang fires. There it is right in front of her: nature, and then something more than nature but taking in no natural thing. Nothing that pure, nothing that beautiful.

Standing next to one of the winter slags, she can smell the vapored water rising through every layer, tangy like sulphur. When it is still hot and dry they are full of branching passages: scores, maybe hundreds of channels of air. Up at the top, in the ridges not strong enough to hold a curl, the mineral edges are brittle and thinner, crenellated. They break into feather-like pieces, bone-white, snowflaked, like the intricate, grittily delicate branches of small dead trees.

Old mine workers have told her about the slag, the hard stories behind all this wavering brightness. She listens to them when Jed is mean or vacant to her and they are all sitting together at the In-and-Out. They describe the way the hot slag would change from day to day and sometimes from shift to shift, depending on the feedstock that went into whatever this gunk and crumble is the byproduct of. Because cold slag can only come from hot, it's nothing more than what cools and settles when the thermal pools lose all of their steam and fire, all of those chains of hydrocarbon lightening.

The men have scars, just like tweakers, little pits and craters of burns they wear like badges from all of the years of standing in front of the naws, which Hadley sees as a long row of orange, bubbling, tongueless serpent mouths. The embers flew out at them like bullets. There were no nets, no grills. The men did not have suits. Later, management came along with aprons made of asbestos. But these would separate with the temperature changes and the front of the things came off their straps and sagged, so more embers came at the unguarded shoulder, each man left with one side of his chest more marked than the other. Sometimes at the In-and-Out, telling these stories, they would pull their T-shirts in by the sleeve holes and show her, looking down, sucking on a cigarette, bent over their cardboard cartons of food.

Some got burned when bad feedstock pushed the product faster, hotter, producing what they called diarrhea slag. It was so hot it was white and wouldn't wait for the hatches to open. It just pushed them out. The little iron door flew forward at them and emptied its rain, its splash of sparking coals. It could be completely liquid, spraying across their skin in streams, as if they'd walked through a sprinkler. These were serious scars, like the giant scars on children trapped in burning houses or car wrecks when the gas exploded: amphibious faces, melted, the features stretched like taffy. Noses and brows that were smooth and pretty rubbed down to nubbins.

The diarrhea slag would happen at their shift's end just when they were most worn out. Their arms were weak and their shovels unsteady, the plates of them spinning around in their hands. They lost an endless amount of time, and had to move from furnace to furnace to stanch the same bad explosive stuff. This feedstock was cheaper. Management cut new corners on the backs and skins of these men, nonunionized and voiceless. You'd see them mostly at fast food joints because they were too ashamed to go out. They would send their wives and kids to do the shopping, or even gas the car.

All around her now the cold slag waits. It is like a single monument to all their years of furious, nullifying work. But at least they were from a time and place where they were making something: vitreous china, porcelains and enamels. Things that people could lift the lids from and sit on and cup their hands above as water ran across their skin and undamaged nails. Their boys, and their Natasha, do something only a little different. The fires and pops—what Jed calls explosions—are sudden and not as expected. They are bigger. They can blow off your fingers and nose and both of your ears. And the product itself is a fiery thing. It cooks in the hollows of the body. It is like the column torches Hadley's father and his friends would build inside the dying elms they had to fell, to help them cave and topple, clearing the lots to build their houses.

It is a fire inside. It's invited in. It is glugged and swallowed like some liquor of hell. The brighter it burns, the bigger the hole. And the greater the ashes and shadows it leaves.

28.

There's a little click, a ticking, a knocking along the veins when it first goes up the chute, when it first gets in under the fine root hairs of the nose. The thirst of the skin inside for it, it makes Hadley think of an egg getting broken and going in the hottest pan, the crackling sides of the thing waiting and seizing and changing the thing, and being changed. The hot, hot transformation at the instant of contact. That quick, that much.

She is taking a taste these days, a spot, which she wouldn't be doing if she didn't know what she was doing with it, know that she is in control. And if it started just when Jed left, then fine, a substitution of one sweet bowl of oblivion for another is fine, just fine.

It's not only things of value that make people happy. What makes people happy, that is the thing of value. Or the bridge between two things of value.

The feeling she has on good powder is one of being plugged in. Currented, turned on. The fast atoms of things invisible and constant, but never once looked for or dreamed of or touched. It is the thing that arrives and *chooses you*. The light down through the leaves, that warms the branches from inside out.

Sometimes there were wires in rooms when Hadley as a kid. Lying around. Cords with their rubber worn off. Some, if she touched them, would knock her right back. But some were just mild humming things, prickling and moving like rivers of bees. A searing, a freeze-burn, like ice water's sting. In the way that it takes her, crank is like this.

Crystal is, of course, its name. It carries the light, its angles and edges.

Once it kicks in, then the feeling is different. Warmer, like turned

on electric blankets. Warmer and warmer, a dial spun rightward—
deep and even and certain as breath.

Sleep is a problem. Sleeping is hard. A washed-out hollowness
stand in for that. All forms of rest get pushed off to one side, like an
old, passed-over piece of her life.

But unconsciousness isn't something she's after. For she now has
all the unconsciousness she needs.

29.

In the night window Hadley watches herself put the safe combination codes into the moraine maps. The reflection is stretched out with one long leg up, skin showing at the ripped knee patch, scratching the numbers from an unfolded small paper onto an unfolded paper half the size of herself with a nodding, slow-moving pencil whose eraser has fallen out. No mistakes allowed. Utmost care. Which is easily taken, given the fact that someone is watching.

The combination numbers are being put on the left top corner of the tint crosses that mark formations. Just like Jed said. One number per cross.

Nice hair, she says, looking up at herself in the glass.

But really, she has to get going with these.

Nice legs. Daddy Long Legs, her Uncle Don used to say.

Hadley wonders where these people—Dun Dun, Ass Man and the other two—get the safe numbers, the algorithms. Jed says it's just a generalized number range, the final product of the formula, and that it takes some "creative amplitude" within that series once they reach it. That's where the true working of the strings comes in, the safe-cracker's creativity. The numbers she's putting in here, they just get them to their final step. To their solo, to the pas de deux.

The numbers go up the cross hatches nicely, birds on a branch, stars on their strings. The pattern she makes with them is the only part that's hers, the numbers an innocent constant and the crosses just parts of what's there, parts of a map no one ever reads. Watching herself in the window, seeing how far from herself she has come, she'll take any pattern or map that will have her, where she can be busy and most alone. It is the design that does it. It is the design that gets her there.

The design is where the doubting stops, and, later, where the terror stops. It's the thing she steps into in making herself.

Nice legs, she says to the girl in the window. She lets her bright hair swing and hang in the dark.

Jed likes it like this, grown out. For a while she had it like Jane Fonda in *Klute*. Fonda's hair then was a copy of some Vietnamese or Cambodian Khmer style—her anti-war days. Jed was right that the style didn't fit Hadley's nose, smaller than Jane Fonda's, or her freckles. She has that skinny, bony, flapping pajama invisibility though. Hadley laughs quickly, like Jane Fonda does, her whole face shooting forward, hand hiding her teeth. Not a bad person to look like. Now Hadley looks like Jane Fonda with her hair grown out, like in later years. Stuck here in the high desert with a pocketful of pens.

Hadley is making a trail, road markers for thieves. All the books she's read let her know that the singing begins in a sadness like this. All songs link into one long one, or the same one being remade like a snake, twisting and flipping onto its back, shaking off the dead skin of an old sadness.

She leans back, lays the pen in a crook of the map. The Hadley in the in the window is doing the same.

It is a design we make, that all these implications become. It curls up into a bridge back over the water we can't look down at anymore. The only doctor for her is Doctor Williams: *It is a design that makes them sing. It is a design.*

30.

This is what she knows:

From where she sits, spotting, Hadley doesn't really have to do anything at all except watch them come out: Dun Dun, Property, Ass Man and Bom, right out the back door, doing what they planned, ding, ding ding.

Jed says that they'll be able to blend right in with people, exiting nonchalantly like normal citizens, having quietly done their work in the vault, the cash room, the safe room, whatever it is, courtesy of Hadley's most unique of terrain maps.

So what is she doing up here? What *would she be doing*, she'd asked Jed. And all he could say was "Spotting." Which means calling them on the cell—no walkie-talkies, like the old bank robbing days—in the event that somebody other than the security guard shows up. A squad car, say. An off-duty E-plate cruiser. Somebody who looks to Hadley's ridiculously untrained eye like a plainclothesman, a flat-foot, a semi-retired G-man. Some guy from the office of the Inspector General, somebody whose professional antennae tells him he's seeing something that needs watching and who, accordingly, needs to put the hammer down on their four artisans.

She moves the binoculars up over the bank roof's sparkling black tarp, littered with bottles, broken canvas stadium seats, piles of newspapers, up to the rim of mountains and far towns that on days like this make North Hollywood the crystal opposite of the sand and fog lands Jed and she drive down here from. The folds and crevices of the peaks' long flanks come out of the air at them like neon sculptures, vivid and twinkling, running from crimson to rusty sassafras and then back to a still, bright, molten gold: a distant, incipient lightning.

The long river of cars still comes down the 101, too, as thick and slow-moving as any earlier hour, still an unmoving egg in the snake's throat even now, 10:15 a.m., the day in full swing. The sky the purest and deepest blue, too, throbbing with color really, like the paint on a polished car.

And people go about their business, not possibly knowing what's going on inside the bank. And how could they, with nothing to arouse their suspicions? And besides, they have their lives to attend to, their incessant business calling them, pulling them, the shit-work of the mundane tugging them along like a fishing rod line, up onto the dry land of their deaths. They look to Hadley like the people in the Balthus painting, walking in the same street, completely ignoring each other, while the workman recklessly swings his plank around close to their heads and the newsboy announces a new war.

The sunshine itself is cold in these high places, these northern burbs. It make the mica sparkle on the sidewalk and the shadows of the people jump uncertainly from their careful gait, narrow spears of taffy wobbling out and back and out again, pooling into invisibility.

There's a clunk at the bank door and Hadley moves the glasses down. At first she thinks it's an old person fainting against the great tinted plate of it, but it's Bom Dia, a long bag in his hand, a workout bag, jammed in the opening so he has to tug at it, angle it differently to get it through. Hadley doesn't think it's cash inside because cash wouldn't have bunched in the door. It's something stiffer, larger.

A man in a suit runs after him, talking on a cell phone and yelling for Bom to stop, waving his free arm. Then behind *him* comes Dun Dun, carrying the same kind of bag with a grey, shiny garment sticking out of it, much the same color and shininess as the sidewalk.

Then comes the bleat—*whomp, whomp*—thunderous, the first gasp of a siren as the squad car drives right up onto the square in front of the bank doors, and Bom and Dun Dun run halfway down the shaded side street fence row and stop. Hadley keeps the binoculars on the cops and with one free eye sees Bom and Dun Dun pulling unknown things out of their unzipped bags, handing stuff to each other.

     RICHARD WIRICK

One of the cops coming out the back sees something that makes him balk, runs back to his car, opens its door and kneels down behind it, reaching to the dash stand to unclip his riot shotgun. The other cop is behind *his* door aiming his pistol with both hands toward Dun Dun.

Bom is out in the middle of the side street in a squarish vest and padded pants. He is aiming a gun, a big machine gun, at the cop with the pistol on the squad car's driver's side. Then a tat-tattling comes out of Bom's gun barrel, yellow muzzle flashes that blast the patrol car's window out and makes the cop scoot lower and lift his legs so his whole body is behind the armored door. He lifts up and fires a double tap back at Bom, his shoulders and hair covered with lime green, stuck-together hunks of glass.

Another squad car pulls up behind this one and cops get out with bigger guns, dressed like Bom and Dun Dun, like grey-painted soldiers lodging the stocks in their ribs and firing at Bom.

There is a bright pink mist, and inside the mist the top of Bom's head comes off completely, opens up like a loose-lidded jar. His whole body lifts up in the air and the gun flies out of his hands, and when he drops, his brains and the blood of his head spill out and splash across the middle of the street.

Dun Dun fires at the cop who killed Bom. The cop grabs his shoulder, blood coming out through the creases of his fingers, and says "FUCK." Dun Dun is behind a tree now, moving his back along the bark, scoping for a clear shot and trying not to look at the blood pumping out of Bom, spreading and deepening on the blacktop.

Property of Jesus is in the doorway now, already dressed in his shooting clothes. Jed said no guns, no cops, no *Keystone Cops*, and here is Prop and probably Ass Man behind him, staring at two cars full of cops, as two more pull up with their lights flashing.

Dun Dun fires more blasts from behind the tree and the rest of Car Number One's windows are out, the windshield too, its sides beginning to fill with patterns of smoking holes. The cops in the third and fourth cars have no special guns or suits and are left to crouch like the first cop, clutching their pistols with their chests heaving.

Dun Dun holds his trigger down, then moves his muzzle back

and forth, spraying fire. Ass Man comes out and runs behind a ledge of the building. When he sees Bom's head on the street, he bends over and pukes, quickly, neatly, then flattens himself up against the building again.

News crews are here, helicopters. Bank robbers aren't supposed to be toting this much stuff. Dun Dun lets off another blast and then a round hits his Kevlar vest, knocking the wind out of him and making him drop to his knees. Then the cops with pistols each fire two quick taps again and Dun Dun takes them in the face.

Dun Dun's forehead and nose peel away, and Hadley holds her breath until he's fallen, crumpled and shriveled up like a sunflower.

But Prop and Ass Man run behind a stopped car, throw the driver out, get behind its doors, and keep the firing up. Property is all bug-eyed but Ass Man is cool, issuing unintelligible instructions above the echo of the firefight, the pings and hisses of ricochets off the bricks and flagstones. Their car must be in neutral because it's drifting forward slightly as they fire, an additional weapon of unintended stealth showboating its way through the confusion.

Then there is an explosion, *two* explosions inside the car. The cops have fired flares or stun grenades that have combined into some big burning ball, and black, black smoke pours out the windows, and Ass Man falls away from it, his clothes on fire.

In the second Prop breaks away and looks down at Ass Man, they fire at him, his arms and head twitching as loops and curls of blood fly through the air, his knees taking the first stage of his fall but then, unable to hold him, letting him tip backwards in the fire soot and ongoing small explosions.

And then it's over. The cops move forward to kick the bodies and check for pulses. Ass Man burns, his flesh charring and wrinkling, the flames licking over his curling hands. A cop stands over him with a fire extinguisher but doesn't turn it on.

Hadley remembers that Ass Man was supposed to be the carrier of her maps. He wasn't hauling a duffel like the others, and so they must have been on him, under his armor.

31.

She pounds on Jed's chest so hard it knocks the wind out of him, and he sits bent over in front of his strange ironing board sculpture, slobber coming out of his mouth that Hadley wants to be blood.

"You *said* NO GUNS," she screams, and when he grunts, laying back, "You said NO ROBBERY."

She repeats back to him his promises, reminding him of their usual worth, the usual dreck she never learns from, and he stays still. The groans coming out of him make Hadley think she's really done some harm this time, something to worry about. But he is the Liar Prince and probably faking.

Jed lifts his hands up for a break, for space.

The hand trembles and goes still. Hadley's guessing it's not from her punch. He's scared too.

She tries again. "Who KNOWS about us? Who knows, and when?"

He draws in two or three long breaths like he does when he's going for emphasis, when he wants what he's about to say to be the final word.

"Nobody," he says. "Nobody knows and nobody's telling. Everybody's scared."

And it *did* make sense that nobody would talk, that the more anybody talked the more trouble there would be. And the Slavs were a unit unto themselves, who would have been working for themselves if Darko's crew hadn't given them a cut.

She's made copies of the maps, three or four actually, but on the magazine's machine at school. Jed said something about needing others for other jobs, and she made them and stashed them all behind one of the file cabinets.

Jed is satisfied with what he's said. Cut one way, looked at from one angle, his eyes are as blue and clear as they've always been. A deep, deep blue, like cottonwood flowers, or the water in summer at Convict Lake where they went one time.

But they're rheumy, too, with a wet grey around the borders. He is quiet, but a quiet that's prickly with rage, the grey laying over a black pool where peace could be, but where Hadley thinks a thrown match—a mood, a gesture of hers—could make the empty space, the wide floor, all of him, burn.

"You said we'd never go with them, with people like that."

She thinks of the other maps, of whether her copies were the only ones. Even if Darko called off all the jobs with the Slavs, he might have made even more copies, where he usually copied things at the Kinkos on Sirrotkin. It would be in the Kodak computer, every bit of what he'd done; the irretrievable, you-are-responsible-for botched solos, everything the enormous enlarger, the rollerized printer pushed out onto the cutting table. He could have tubes of them any-where, and they would be imprinted on the machine's hard drive, like million-year-old trilobites in granite.

Jed is shaking his head to say that Darko took all of them, all the copies she gave Jed, and they burned up with Ass Man, like letters thrown in the fireplace.

He sinks into the brown Tibetan pillow. Its checkering folds around him like a net.

The plea in his eyes has shifted. Something in their texture, their color, tells Hadley he isn't even trying to get her to understand. He's grieving for himself. And he's afraid of something: being alone with the dosage he's up to, stuck inside his Darko juggernaut, something. Maybe just being without her. For just this moment, at least, Hadley realizes that she is in control. The power has jumped just now, down through her eyes and spreading along her veins and skull like a good snort settling through the blood, sticking to the neurons.

Whatever the underlying causes, the light is going out in him, and he wants her hands around the flame, a cone of sheltering fingers around what dwindles. It's moments like these where she thinks she'll be open to an impromptu lurch, a blind embrace, whatever she thinks

     RICHARD WIRICK

he might be holding out hope for. She imagines it will be the key to the mystery they make of each other, and which will somehow be figured out in a time of solitude, darkness, the two of them hidden together.

But she resists. For this moment there's only the conviction that there is no key, and there is no mystery. They are like two animals thrown together on the same road, running away in the same direction. They smell each other, they circle each other. Need and fear have made them what they are, and there is nothing else.

III

32.

For days after the bank job, it dominates the news. It gets much more airplay than the normal armed robbery, because of the sophistication of the Russians' weapons and armor. The police had been outgunned at first, and were lucky to be in North Hollywood, which is zoned for gun shops, one of which they burst into and whose owners—watching everything on live feed on monitors over their heads—took out fully automatic machine guns they weren't supposed to have or sell. They filled the cops' arms with the things: AK-47s, Tec 9s, Mannlicher-Carcanos with 21-round banana clips and double springed reloads, better vests, visors and helmets, the works. Hadley turned on the news that night and there it was: Dun Dun stepping out into the middle of the street in his moon suit and spraying fire, whirling his muzzle back and forth until the cop's round hits his forehead and all of him becomes a grey-red cloud.

Hadley's anxiety, her using, just everything now makes her go back to those four, putting herself down into their skins and imagining what it must be like to be ready for death, primed for it, looking down the barrel as the cold, slow seconds follow each other. Does time really slow down in those moments? Like everything being under water and the sounds being deeper, stretched out into a slowed tape, a taffy-morph of flattened words? All gunfights are surrounded by a kind of shock wave, a dense thickening of the air that lets you stay focused and alert, but at the same time makes each action hyper-analyzable, drawing tremendous attention to its detail.

What were they thinking, too, when they were down on the ground wounded, the ones whose heads didn't immediately explode, like water balloons? All of *that* was on TV, in still photos too, the wounded ones lying there, wedged under tires and fenders, still clutching the guns with their faces eerily visible, flesh and blood men dying of their wounds, as men had died in wars for a thousand years.

And what does it feel like to have the life seeping out of you, the consciousness slipping away like trickles from a drain pipe? Besides the pain, is it any different than going under for a wisdom tooth? Does the screen go grey, the edges of your sight blacken and the black move in toward the center? After-images rolling across the darkness, life flashing, like they say, before your eyes? Or are you numb, half-conscious, scrambled, able to see but not move or speak, the neurons missing each other in their flickering, supernatural spray of electrical specks?

Hadley imagines death now in those moments like she's always imagined it—a deepening cold, a barely perceptible rising of frigid, slightly dirty cistern water, soaking cell by cell and pore by pore through your wet warm flesh. And as it switches off, as the waves of chill take her under, and if it occurs to her that it was an error that flattened her there in the gravel and blood-muck, she imagines her last thought is of an enormous irreversible swindle: that every mistake in her life was one that she could have repaired, erased away, except for the one she'd just made.

33.

She's got the zaps today, starting just when she's looking at some of the new submissions in the magazine office. The zaps make her vision crinkle and surge and the blood inside her head starts to whirl, roaring sometimes like a far off storm, like thunder. It happens when she stops using for a day or two and her brain brain is pleading for a boost, a bridge hit, a carry-over. Crank is its new food and its hunger is as close as anything to actual famishment.

If she's moving, either walking or driving, the zaps get even more interesting, pushing her both inside and out, so she reaches a crisp, steady velocity that's both horribly scary but completely controlled. Her neurons are in the water now, the sweet elixir, a rain of dopamine on their thirsty heads, sucking and gusting, blowing and swirling. And when she's moving, she *is* the motion, the space she's moving through, the clearness and emptiness of its air, its very endlessness.

All of which makes Hadley want to go, to get somewhere. But she's got manuscripts to read, a pile of them stacked criss-cross under the corner window, waiting for the unforgiving blue pencil. She picks one of them up but can't read any of it. The words, however smooth and moving, scatter like fish in the tank when she taps on the glass. She turns a page over and starts to doodle. Doodling, eating, screwing, driving. It is all alive here in the ether, its airy soil feeding any one of them she chooses.

Two or three figures down, Hadley realizes she's drawing a column of *chakras*, the reincarnation objects explained to her once by Jed, in turn explained to him by Harish, the juice man at the Karnateka Café. (The Karnateka, in a gentrifying strip of shops in Panorama City, was described in the *Weekly* once as the benighted region's "only stop on the Godhead line.")

The *chakra* column is a sort of totem pole, each section separated, of one's possible re incarnation vessels, animate and inanimate, hideous or breathtakingly pretty. Hadley went through a Balinese catalog of them from Harish's spinning magazine rack. She'd looked at groups of them, four or six to a page, and what she was drawing now was a hodgepodge of what she'd spotted flipping through them the first time. What someone would turn into in the next cycle wasn't so much predetermined as pre-*screened*: certain things were culled and certain ones tossed, all with no apparent logic, by the panoply of gods, who themselves seemed juiced-up, cranked-up, steroided versions of this off season circus: monkeys and bats, bug-eating plants, mufflered princes and sub-zero amphibians, and what looked like lions or flickering suns with lion faces, vacant and calmed.

They had all, in their Hindu stoner riffs, guessed at what they'd come back as: what mythical beast, what hybrid flora. She slips the doodled page back into the manuscript, realizing she'll have to Xerox that sheet and make notes on *it*, unless she wants the writer to know the truth: that half the reader's mental space is reverie, meandering blankness, unfocused little foglets of thought.

She starts down the stairs remembering the fun of this guessing game, the commentary on one another's choices, what instinctual predilections say about the laughing, guessing choosers. Her arm is half asleep, as she trails it on the handrails; she shakes it to get the tingling out. She knows that Vedic doctrine lets humans come back not just as animals or things, but also as just another human, suffering even more for the screw-ups with which she'd stuffed her generously allotted, karma-repairing time.

When Hadley gets home, her mother is at the kitchen table reading the paper. The robbery is still on the front page. The still she saw on the evening news two nights ago is there: Prop's face, with a big screen cowboy's details of sweat and wrinkles and cinders, staring out from the giant tire his cheek is wedged against.

34.

Her Mom's eyes have that dreadful, edgy cold they always do when she wants to talk, and she bends the paper down from where it covers her face to let it flap under her chin, like it is a hot day and she is fanning herself. She's been reading the robbery story, obviously, and though she couldn't make any connection between the Russians and Hadley and Jed, she gives the nod to everything she says as if she's onto something.

"Saw Natasha's Mom at the Costco. The grafts are taking and she won't be as scarred as they thought. It's all down in the…." She lifts her hands above her Mu-Mu, "…the neck, the top of her collarbone."

Hadley sits down and takes the Metro section.

"And it gets better. They give injections…to smooth the scarring out."

She wants Hadley to know she knows more about these things than Hadley ever could, because of her age, her being a mother.

Hadley is starting to flatten, the zaps pooling and rippling away from the edges of the frame her seeing makes. And the hairs of her skin feel just like that, flattened, tapering away, like the line in the Donne poem about "gold to airy thinness beat."

"You're nervous, honey. What's wrong?"

"Nothing."

"Is Jed driving that truck?" she asks, shaking her head, holding back the sigh. "The things we do for money. Look at these people."

Hadley puts the paper down, looking at the picture of Prop. The Metro section has something about utility rates, rollbacks, how energy traders have been cheating entire cities on their electrical grids, whole sections of the country. Hadley always thought the government controlled the keepers and dispensers of something that basic.

But it's her mother who has the jitters, the deep creeps, what her father used to tease Hadley with by calling it the "yim-yams." Her eyes and skin, the hair on her arms, are filled with a neediness. Hadley can almost see the hair growing out of her goose bumps, stiffening with static electricity. The iMac is up beside her, beside the seasoning rack, the whitish sleeplight pulsing under the keyboard.

Hadley's mother watches Hadley looking at it, then looks at it herself, then back at Hadley. "Jed needs to get himself anchored, honey. I know that. I know that." She takes a deep, uneven breath. "Who doesn't know that?"

Hadley spins the Metro section around and around. The sun is coming in and warming the wallpaper to the point where, here in the high desert, it will start to bubble, like linoleum did in the old, yellow house.

"But he's something. He's got potential. Nothing a little working on won't fix."

This is the way Hadley's mother looks in Hadley's direction now, the full measure of her diminishment hitting Hadley like a blast of dust. She is not supposed to hope for anything better, only to be measured by what she has and what she might wish for. Women, all of them, lucky to catch whatever they could.

Hadley wants to blame her mother's generation. But it's not that simple. She has friends—not many now, but she's had them—with mothers whose message is to reach, to stretch, to grab anything that's *not* a man to make yourself. It was their gospel and their blessing. It was the program for their daughters, the next step up the matrilineal ladder.

Hadley's mother glances back up toward the counter, at the sleeping iMac screen. "You know I don't weigh in on these things. That much." An alarm, a timer is going off somewhere. It beeps six or seven times, stops, then starts again. "I try not to."

"I know you don't."

"I try not."

"You grill me sometimes, but not on this. Not on men."

"It's hard to know when to talk. You know? You'll know some day. When you have kids."

"You can spy sometimes. You've grilled me."

"I worry about the big things, what can hurt you." She is looking down at the picture of Prop's head under the wheel, looking straight out, the treads mixed up with his bloody hair, his eyes showing he knows where he is, between worlds.

Hadley sees the film of sweat on her mother's lip. Sees her eyes start to dart, like something is crawling up her leg, creeping up over her. She wants Hadley out, wants to get back to what she was doing.

"I'm just saying," Hadley's mother says, "that he's a good boy. There's worse. If you're going to end up leaving, that has a lot to do with it. Whether he's somebody you'd, well…."

The beeping is softer, clear as a jay's whistle in the trees.

"Whether he's somebody you'd want to go with. But there's worse. That's all I'm saying."

Hadley wants to oblige her, mad as she is. Meaning she just wants to get out of her way now, let her get back to whatever. She gets up from her chair and feels the last clear, even surges of the crank, its sweet residue, the final sprinklings.

She thanks her mother for talking. Hadley cannot blame her for her thwartedness, which in anybody else would blind her, would make her boil. She can't blame her any more than she could blame someone for being inside their own skin, behind their own eyes. Time tells us what we are, how little control we have over our making.

Hadley's mother tells her to take care and to come back later.

Once Hadley is out of the room, she quickly looks back, just a peek, like the peeks her mother spies on her with, and sees her moving her chair over to the Mac. The screen switches on, and the two hands of poker swim up out of their green background.

35.

Hadley is straightening now, flattening, smoothing the zaps out with a long swash of time and water, like the dough spreading under the rolling pin her mother used to let her push and pull from her seat on the high, end-up crate. There's a calm that comes, a deep and even tranquility. *Anenka*, one of the Russians called it.

The submissions are good this time. One story she likes a lot, about a woman cocktail party murderer: strychnine or cyanide she puts in the biscotti of a rival for her star-eyed Teutonic donut empire widower. No one suspects her because of her mentoring, 12-Step past, nobody *that* dedicated to assistance could dispatch anybody from the world. But she does it, this bit of business, leaving the proceedings with her fingerprint-absorbing handkerchief dropped like a feather into her clutch bag.

There's some poetry, too, which isn't Hadley's forte. The Columbian girl from Composition knows poetry. Hadley thinks she needs a poetry editor. She thinks the Columbian girl will be it.

She lays the manuscripts down and wipes off her reading glasses, wondering why she needs them this young. There's no reflection this time in her cubby window, just the dust and cars of the day along 146. The long-slanting dusty light. The dreadful light.

Here's another story. A "Tale," the author calls it, and it does have that kind of cobwebby Poe chill that sends up must and puffs of black dust. The narrator is a ball of mismatched, misplaced tissues (bone, flesh, hair, called a *hamartoma* in medicine, she guesses they *do* exist). But this one speaks from out of a jar on a shelf like Beckett's Unnamable, only angrier, less resigned and adjusted, lurching, popping its lips and "jigging"—the writer is a Welsh girl—"all up and about." She renders the face so crisp and vivid, but with minimal features, that Hadley thinks of little Japanese cartoon blobs with boiling Hannibal Lecter brains and teeth grafted on. Teeth tissue, yes. The creature has lots.

When she's crossing out a section, Hadley starts to crash from the crank: it can happen this late, this far out of the zaps and into your smooth-down, your flattening. It's like wind, hellish strong wind, cold, coming against your bare chest. It knocks and knocks at her. She leans over and falls back. She feels it come for her heart, the main machine, blasting it straight out of her, right through her back ribs and out into the weather.

She cries. For anything or for nothing. She cries for the City, for herself and Jed, for the strange warrior-editor she's replacing, for Natasha and her rubbery new homemade skin. She cries for her father at his easel and her mother at her gambling screen.

When Hadley brings her hands away from her face, the tears are down past her palms, on her wrists, still running, like raindrops on glass. Jed is coming over. She thinks of two things: how red her eyes are, and how nothing he does or says in these times can make her better.

36.

Some of Darko's new friends, not long after the robbery, started new money-making schemes, new "PJs' they called them, which Hadley eventually learned was short for projects. Neither Darko's friends nor Darko came anywhere near Jed with these ideas. No overtures, which relieved her no end. They all heard about them later on down the line, along the work route—in the washing houses and the cooking sheds, driving the trucks. Sometimes they'd hear about the more outrageous ones at parties, or dinners of the four of them: Hadley and Jed, Darko and his sometimes girlfriend Lidija (pronounced "Lydia"). If the project was truly, truly crazy, it would make the papers, though never the *Times*. It would be the big item in the Palmdale *Gazette* or the O.C. *Register*. Or one of those crappy Inland Empire papers, really just a giant packet of coupons with a couple of pages of local news slipped in.

These friends of Darko's, friends from Serbia, had been influenced by bigger brothers, or bigger brothers' or sisters' friends. Their older siblings left what was then an intact Yugoslavia and traveled up and West, to Paris, Amsterdam, London. They were political. They read Italian revolutionary philosophers, Marxists and communards from the northern Mediterranean cities and from places like Trieste and Madrid. Many of the philosophers had been in prison and had written their books—small pamphlets, really—in the cells of jails and holding tanks, places of intense interrogation and long months, sometimes years, of isolation.

The political people mixed with artists, absurdists, anarchists. They were seekers of visual chaos and chaos in the order of life. They were contemptuous of family, occupations, the struggles and hierarchies of status. All of them, individuals and movements, had names that seldom translated out of the mysteries of their own language. The movements, these mixtures of art and politics, all reached a pitch in the mid-to-late Sixties. They crested in the very early Seventies, and by the middle of that decade they sprang up everywhere, their only signifiers being violent, incredibly absurd actions that seemed half terror, half slapstick comedy. They were called the Situationists, the Arcanas, the Feelies, the Weepies. The latter two names show how awkwardly the monikers—even though proper names sometimes— came over into English from the Dutch or Italian or German.

The "actions," as they were called, could never be mistaken for anyone else's. They were completely unique, like snowflakes, finger- prints, voice patterns. But they had a sort of family resemblance in their humorous outrageousness, and linked themselves together into a chain of sloppy, powerful direction. Tweakers, who modeled them- selves on the Situationists in particular, were proud of the surprise they created and the money they brought in from each of the actions. Sometimes no profit came from whatever was done. But the message was deeper and clearer: be afraid, we will be back. There will be more and you can never make yourselves ready for it.

The whole pattern of the Tweakers' actions cut a wedge through the grey, monochromatic days of that Spring, like the quick scrape of a trowel through concrete. One of Darko's friends called the long parade of them something quite the opposite of this. He was more art than politics. He called it a palette. Once at dinner, staring at Hadley, he said it with a click of the tongue against the top of his mouth— "PA-latte"—looking at her as if wondering if she were old enough to understand the pun. Actually, she was probably the only one at the table who got it.

Among the various actions on the palette were these:

Requisitioned paratrooper outfits from an Army-Navy store in Eagle Rock and stormed into a free clinic in Venice, demanding opiates, barbiturates, things that had street value and that they could unload in the alleys downtown, between the *schmatta* district and Skid Row. Of course, much of this stuff was just kept. Everybody liked Vikes, Percocets. If one of the Tweakers was a meth user himself, he called opiates the "Go Slows," which one of the Nigerian kids said was the name for traffic jams in Lagos.

Went into a rich fraternity at USC where everybody had just paid their dues in cash, some kind of house rules, and stood over the Pledge Daddy with a club until he opened the safe, pulled out the shoebox, and dug his fists into the rolls of twenties and fifties. The bi-quarterly dues were modest—$350 per pledge—but the Kappa Sigs were taking in more pledges to stay afloat after a hazing incident (the first actual butt-chugging death) drove up the cost of their liability insurance. The Tweakers stuffed five Carl's Jr. bags with cash and then kicked the Pledge Daddy, a big Texan who had been interrogating the grunts in a basement dungeon, in his fairly well-developed stomach. Some political justification was offered because they were an old frat from the genteel Upper South, Duke, U.VA., Vanderbilt and so on, and the first honorary president of the frat was Jefferson Davis. The Tweakers threw a sugar pot against the portrait of him above the fireplace and it emptied in a long, white swath—mistaken for something else—across his brown (not gray) double-breasted coat and ascot.

Robbed a payday loan shop on Pico and Lincoln Boulevard, right across from Santa Monica High, where armed (!) school-crossing guards could have stopped them. This was especially tough because most predatory lenders supposedly had thicker plexiglass than regular banks. Someone Darko knew stuck a P38 up into the hole under the window and, apparently, it fit perfectly. When the lady put her hands up, he shouted at her to put them down and empty the register. She asked what a register was (he'd heard the line from a movie, he was nineteen) and he said "where the money is, the computer." One of the Tweaks had to pee and was afraid to go to the Subway next door, too close to the school and grounds, and so he unloaded in the wastebaskets full of wire receipts for the money the laborers and cleaning ladies send home. The take: $18,000 and change.

Beat up and stole the house take of a band at a downtown club, the revitalized Flaming Colossus. The band was the Hostage Wives. The rumor was that the players, all actually men, were on their way to a Beverly Hills restaurant to hobnob with celebrities and Mayor Villa-grossa. The Tweakers grabbed the lead singer, Hoke-A-Do, a kind of Arab manque, out of the limousine and pulled him down the stairs of the old stock exchange building next to the club. This action was one of the more political and far less aesthetic numbers. It was like what one of Darko's older cousins said the SDS, the Weathermen, did with the Chicago Police in the Sixties in the Days of Rage. One guy pushed a detective through a Gucci store plate glass window on Michigan Avenue. Someone had thrown a Molotov cocktail in before the push and black smoke flowed out of the gold creased frame of the doorway. The cop was screaming inside. Nothing artistic about it.

Truck hijackings, more often without guns than with them.

"It is amazing," Jed said once, "how much robbery you can accomplish without a firearm." It made Hadley think, of course, about Jed, an offhand comment like that. Maybe he had just been watching some TV news. But the hijackers were all business, pinpointed, very intelligently agendized. Boxes and long panel sheets of pure ephedra on their way to antihistamine assemblers. The pure stuff, intercepted between manufacturer and pharmaceutical endpoint. Couldn't have been more perfect. There was a video of it. The Tweaks were just pounding their palms with their clubs, standing there like Keystone Cops. The stuff in long brown boxes like the one shutters come in, the men pulling a couple of sheets out just to check, the silvery cardboard wobbling in the sunlight like a kite about to be picked up and run with. But it just slid back in. Liquid gold. Spansules of gold. Not a lot of cash value but got around the volume limits on the over-the-counter medicine purchases that make you have to run from county to county like a…well, like a criminal. But they wanted everyone to know—the truck job or jobs, which had to mean they videoed it themselves. So some art there. The camera rolling. Truly an action, with a capital "A."

Smashed in the window of a pharmacy in Westwood, a particularly snotty one, a Hortense and Converse. Usually they would go for a place with more over-the-counter inventory, like a Rite-Aid or a CVS, but there was your politics—a bourgeois pharmacy asking for it, getting it, saying "Hit me. The little people can't afford to come here." The thick glass lay all over the street like the snow you see by the side of the road just coming into the mountains. Chunks of it as big as fists, as fat as crumpled up pieces of paper down at the mag office. Hadley could imagine the Tweaks coming out with armloads of boxes, or having gone in back to get bulk containers, true sweet booty, take-care-of-you abundance, make-your-raid-leader happy volume. Maybe they had a truck of their own, a U-Haul sheathed in black, and if bulk inaccessible, locked behind grates like the opiates now. They probably just used shopping carts or those hand baskets that always have stuff still stuck to the bottom. They ran out through the empty starburst of the window, their arms piled high with rattling, clattering six by eight inchers falling out of the basket tops, all of the escapees orderly, avoiding running over each other. Again, with this one, the cash value impossible to calculate because it was the stuff itself, the badly quickly, what Darko's hippie uncle called, in his acid days, the Genuine Owlsley.

Acquired SSI (State Disability) checks from a group of shelter women, still hooked on opiates, in exchange for Vikes and Dilaudid capsules the Tweaks had no real use for. It was almost, they say, like the waiting room at City of Angels, with the women lining up to cash their checks at a Papa Dough next door to the Dunkin Donuts, where the men handed out little baggies of pills in exchange for the counted-out low denominations. They stuffed the wads of cash in their jackets and, for some reason, ran up onto the roof and did a kind of rain dance, something the Hopis would have done a hundred years ago, though completely out of sight of anybody on the street. One of the Tweaks had to have been buzzed because he crashed his station wagon into one of the girls' cars and just kept going, but then came back and handed her a couple hundred dollars, not enough, with hands that were shaking so much he looked like he was throwing confetti, scattering ashes, though in the state of things you can guarantee, Jed told Hadley, that he was the comparatively manageable picture of composure. They tried it a week later at another SSI outlet, but two black and whites were parked out front, the officers up on stools in the donut shop. The cops in that part of town are not to be messed with, pear-shaped and weighted down with electrical gizmos and doodads like the kind cop listening to the runaway kid in the Norman Rockwell picture. Most were football players at La Cañada or Glendale High, then the Army. If you were filling a space capsule or test plane out at Edwards, you would be able to pack four Tweakers' bodies into one policeman's. Gravity, balance, weight distribution. The right stuff.

Did another pretty brazen, all-out action film kind of robbery, knocking over a Wells Fargo on La Cañada Boulevard right as the place opened and the Brinks truck had been in the day before. They wore wigs and big butterfly patterned sunglasses like Jewish ladies from the Valley. They used P38s, the weapon of choice of the Seventies Situationists, because they are short-barrelled and you can hold them right at your breastbone, in the middle of your chest, aim it from there without extending your arm and making a suspicious profile for anyone driving by. Easier to give orders this way—you don't have to worry about how you look to anybody except the person who is going to do your, perhaps loudly communicated, bidding. This was a bank on one of the grubby South Valley boulevards, an old Okie neighborhood. There were junkies and winos and teenage whores out front with wild, hollow eyes. Everyone's eyesight would be too rheumy to see or remember; bad witnesses, good passersby. This Tweak group had an escort of bikers, and the whole jittery group blazed away in a gaggle of soot-chugging, thunderous exhaust, the valves and hatches on the older bikes clanging away like submarine ports, the saddle bags filled with unfired small pistols and plastic trays of reloads.

37.

Jed thinks that, six weeks later now, enough time has passed. He wants to take the maps to a new group of Russians in Bonnie Doon, give them the algorithms, and let them open the vaults of just a few of the Clovis County banks, maybe Santa Cruz too.

His arms are crossed on the back of the chair. He tips it toward Hadley. Can he do this because he's high, because his brains are scrambled from being high for so long, because hopefulness when you're high is just this: blind motion and hovering, the distance to the ground not mattering?

"I'm assuming you won't hear me out?"

"Didn't say that."

"So you will."

His palm-scratching milder now, but still there. He lifts the scratching finger up quickly, up out of his pocket as if he's just touched a hot coal.

"I'm ears."

Hadley still has the zaps, she knows, or she wouldn't have left a word out like that.

"I'm all ears."

Her hands itch, too, and she moves them across each other, scraping them along the inside of her forearms.

Jed has a left eye wandering now. The powder can loosen the eyes, the feel of them inside the head. It loosens the way they look, the way they come across to a careful viewer, which means another user.

"How are the stories going?"

"Great," Hadley says. "Lots to pick through. Lots to see."

"You the boss now?"

She follows the roving eye, remembering the Bowie album with one brown, one blue.

"Depends on whether we get Timmy back."

"Jesus." He winces.

"Well," Hadley says. "It *is* Iraq. But he could also get posted some-where else."

"There's a couple of places the new group of Russians picked out." He pauses a minute and then says, "Romanians, actually."

"What are you going to do?"

"I'm not—"

"What. Are."

Hadley leans forward and puts her fingers on the chair's edge.

"You. Going…."

"—Nothing."

"Nothing like always? Nothing like…like giving the cash to Dun Dun?"

"Yeah. That *was* nothing. No tracing. No searches and matches. The job didn't work is all."

"Is all."

"Hadley," says his mouth, says his orbiting eye. "Tell me again why the maps can't be traced."

"Cause the copies are with us. In those tubes. At the office."

"Those guys were gone *over*, Jed. The cops searched their clothes. Their pockets. Their jackets."

"Here," he says, pointing to his head, "is where the scrips were. Committed. To memory."

"Why did I embed them then? What the fuck?"

"They're smart people. They're Russians. They memorize things. Yuri told me they memorize pages and pages of things before they're even in kindergarten."

"But."

"But they can forget, like anybody."

Jed turns the chair around, and it's tipped up when his butt hits the seat. The legs slam down hard.

"If you're up for it, we can take them the maps. The embeds. Every copy. Every one."

"We? Where *we* going?"

"To the town. To be there. Offer moral support."

There is the faint hurt around Hadley's heart, the slow circle of bruising. LIke the halo, blue and deadly, on a campfire stove's burner. With the zaps, or what's left of them, the feeling is stronger. It's like the pulsing of an open cut, the dark sparkle of a wound.

"Darko just wants us. He said he'll need spotters. He offered traceless card phones. I told him nothing doing. I think he wants you there, if they need it, to run them through the patterns."

"The great memorizers? But *they're* the safecrackers. They need *me* to hide their numbers in the...?"

"...weeds?"

Hadley lifts her finger. "The moraines. Beneath the weeds. What the weeds grow out of."

"They just need you, Had. *Need* you. Need *me*. All the peripherals. They need the small planets, the ones outside the telescope. And yeah, they can't remember every single sequence. The maps are refreshers."

Jed lights up a Djarum. It gives his fingers something to do besides scratching.

"There was a story I read today," she says, "about an African in the States. From the bush. I mean a *pygmy*."

His face is puzzled. the smoke hangs, blue and solid, right over him.

"He sees an escalator. He gets on it. By the time he figures it out, understand how it works, he's ready to get off. The whole fucking thing's over."

The smoke gets thicker, a horizontal cloud that deepens with each exhale. Its end starts to curl, his good luck quarter moon. Its bottom tapers to something sharp and clean.

"Only he doesn't just get off. He's a *pygmy*. He stumbles. Two nails from his feet are torn away by the steps. He sits at the top, no one helping. His nails come around again and again, just like that...." she makes a roundabout with her hand. "Just like that, *tick tick tick*."

He cuts his hand through the smoke. The cloud of it curls into itself, rises.

"I've lost him," Hadley thinks. She's still saying "*tick tick*," whispering it into the blue.

     RICHARD WIRICK

38.

They found Mary Langley today. She was in her car, parked in Trillium Canyon. A couple of days of dust on the windshield and one of the wipers was halfway up, the other one apparently not working. It took them four hours, because the paramedic truck got blocked by a tree that had fallen in the short time they were down there with the stretchers.

Mr. Langley had put out a missing person report on her, but he had not really kept track of her since she had started using and eventually disappearing for long stretches with the men she was using with. He would hear about her from other people. He would hear about her from their kids, who he saw sometimes at the college. But when she came back to the house and took off with one of his trucks, one with a toolbox he hadn't bolted to its bed, and it had gone on to four or five days, eight days, he put in the call. He had an idea of what had happened.

People can hit a level with the powder, but once they start shooting, they peak pretty quickly, they crest, and then they have to keep going at that altitude because their nerves are on fire and need the quick dowsing that only a bloodstream shot can give them.

That's when the sexual craving sets in, a frantic, doglike lust that makes people drop their tasks and duties and peel off their companion's clothes like badgers in dirt, like moles in the moist, warm earth. It is like that—hungry and immediate and filthy. People have left children in laundromats with strangers to fuck standing up in supply rooms, surrounded by wheeled buckets and piles of hangers and disinfectant fumes. They have left retarded adult brothers to circle the block while going at it the back seat of old, large, cars in full daylight, with the windows cracked to keep them from steaming. Real estate agents screw their clients on the wood floors of houses they are show-ing; what man would turn down a beautiful showing broker once she opens her blouse and presses herself around his face? People fuck their dealers and their dealer's drivers, their children's teachers, their spouse's sisters and their own sisters and total strangers they see across a check-washing trough, pausing for a half-second to look through the drying paper at somebody they know is having the same thought, the same incessant conflagration.

The energy is unbelievable, the stamina. If these people could be turned into soldiers, trained in the desert with the stuff, they would fight like rats on dopamine. Sex with Jed like this is jackrabbit sex. He is so up, hard for hours. Sometimes Hadley is sore and has to turn him away. Sometimes she bleeds.

But if she has had a taste, they go forever, for hours like distem-pered creatures, their sweat dripping on each other like hot grease. Their hearts are pounding, pounding. They feel like they are going to black out. The narcotic release in their crotches fans out through their bodies like blooming extraterrestrial pods. But still they are nothing like the others, the ones who latch onto each other the way that drowning, clutching people do. There is no love. There is no con-tentment. There is nothing but a snatching, a feverish dynamism and blindness.

Mrs. Langley was with whom?—a number of people, a number of men right after her habit hit high gear. Hadley saw her one day when she was getting some tile with her father at J & B Acoustical. Mrs. Langley was with a guy who looked like Tom Waits, right down to the goatee and tattered jacket and pieces of straw sticking to his collar and elbows. He was dragging a space heater along the floor, and she followed, pushing a blue plastic wicker shopping cart. The cart was empty. She wore a stiff, dirt-caked mackinaw and her eyes were bruised. She definitely had the shake.

The next guy Hadley saw her with was the Cloverdale guidance counselor, Mr. Maybee, who wasn't a user but whose wife had just left him and who was hugely grateful for the crazy, nonstop screwing. Here was, essentially, the male ideal: enthusiastic, athletic sex with no requisite discussion afterward. He was flabbergasted and stuck around until she made a sharp turn in the school parking lot while dropping him off, and he was thrown from the passenger door up against a cyclone fence.

After that her mates were mainly dealers, because she would be so quick to get it in her and so amped with desire afterward that she shattered all over them both like a thin, brittle Christmas tree ball, the slightest touch, the slightest pressure blasting everything into rinds and shards. Her car was parked a lot at the IGA or in the alley behind the vegetable market. She didn't try to hide the score, and didn't make much of an effort hiding what came afterward.

She froze to death alone in the car, forgetting how low the temperature could get on a high desert night.

When they bring an OD.B. up from one of the canyons, it is labeled just like that: the "O" and "D" together, as if they are a single unit, with the period following them, then the "B" following the first period and off by itself, as if it really *were* an isolated, lost body separated from the rest of the world, and then followed finally by its own period. Sometimes it seems as sinister as any of the old acronyms like "DOA." But the "B" there, the letter that should be the most frightening, can sometimes seem so benign. It can look like a lost balloon floating.

When they bring an OD. B. up from one of the canyons, they only keep one of the siren lights on, the blue one, and since their passenger is dead, they can drive as fast as they want.

39.

On the nights Hadley thinks the stuff—little of it that she's used—has worked itself out of her, and her blood and bones feel as clear as high desert air, and all trace of the zaps and their attendant conditions are gone, these are the nights when she has the dream of the bees. They are in a comb she's passed to through an inward-opening door of paper or drape that closes behind her with a sense of continuous, constant permeability. Down inside, in the place that brims and descends and where no clear thing keeps itself, come the first of their even murmurings.

The spinning is what she sees before anything else, like the far-whirling wheels that pull her forward into a night carnival. It could be one large body, or a pair, or two, moving like that, a single thing that twirls from the center outward and then back in, the littlest squares of black and yellow widening out and back with the neatness of zipper's teeth. The tinniness of the clattering is what gets her attention most, what pulls the looker into the deeper, lower, brown-shake portions of the hive. And that's when she sees it: the circles of workers, the infinitesimal, spinning robot bodies and smooth black olive heads topped with thin and bending antennae. This is where the mindless circle and crawl of all of them begins, where the cargo of pollen is dropped into pipes and alleys that push it along toward liquidity, to where it becomes the slow-moving river of gold.

The drones take over then, with a louder, motorized fat throbbing, carrying lumps and crumbs of pressed-together cake in front of themselves like another part of their bodies, extra heads put on for sheer, incessant and unquestioning determination. The cakes and crumbs are prizes, special bricks of the eventual monument. No two talk to each other here, but all are talked to by the pattern of their climbing, winding, pulling forward and following of their charges, the constant handing off and taking on.

The Queen looks down on everything. She is the one that starts and ceases, switches everything that surrounds her like some telepathic lever. She's the beginning note, the white fire from the cloud that feeds the lightning rods. Her hum is the hum of mind, the light and guide. Her signals are absorbed by everything.

It's here that the humming takes Hadley over, covers her like a hood and keeps her from moving away. She feels the sheet of bodies on her face, the fur of them against her cheeks. To live is to vibrate just like this. And to die is somehow, also, to come back to just this thing.

When the humming is loudest is when she wakes up. She walks to the shower and turns on the hot. Each droplet of water is like an eraser, erasing away the body of a bee.

40.

Hadley doesn't know Tim's mother. But when the Army men came to tell her about Timmy, she invited them in and made sure she got down into a seat quickly. They are Oklahoma people, or descendants of Oklahoma people, who had suffered in the Dust Bowl. They were practical people. Timmy was a practical person.

But she let out a wail and fell over in the chair. This is what Natasha's Mom told Hadley's. But how could she have known? Who could have told her that? Nobody, certainly not the Army officers. They leave, it is said, right after they deliver the news. It's when they come in pairs that you worry. Every car that comes up a road, the people look closer now.

Maybe one of the neighbors saw the car go up the road and watched. There would have had to have been an open window, or someone in one of the neighbor's houses, farther away, could have looked through binoculars.

Hadley's mother called about five minutes after one of the magazine staffers had told Hadley. She wanted to know exactly what the staffer said, but Hadley said she couldn't talk, she was going right out the door to somewhere.

She couldn't believe how quickly it happened to him. He had been there about three months. He'd circled the date he was to leave and somebody had torn that page off the calendar and put it in one of the left-hand drawers of the editor's desk.

They'd made him an officer, he'd told his mother, because they said he had a leader's bearing. The term they used for it was Command Presence. He'd had it at the magazine, but Hadley thinks he figured that in war, this war at least, it would have grown into something hugely important, something he could build on back in civilian life, whatever he chose to do. War is like yeast, Castiglione said. It's like a hot house where strains of greatness and fortune grow, strains that might stay undernourished in normal life.

But life was over for Tim now. Why didn't anybody stop him? Especially his father, who had been in Vietnam. But maybe that was it. He was probably one of the ones who saw his time there as a crucible, and then raised his son to believe the military was the highest of callings, a profession almost preordained.

The truth was that Hadley hadn't even tried to talk him out of it. She was so busy with her own life's strange turnings, all the stupid problems with college and Jed. She'd made no effort. She was surprised at how fast he'd enlisted and was in, and was there. It was like a conveyor, with the near end catching him, a corner of his shirt, pulling him down and onto the flat, moving slaughter line.

The day he'd told Hadley, she saw what she thought was a pleading in his eyes. But how could she have known that's what it was? He stood in the hall between the magazine office and the provost's lounge. She imagined he wanted to be talked out of it because she couldn't imagine anyone, any human being, wanting to go. But no two can know the same, even as they look into each other's eyes, and there was the other force driving Tim—his father—telling him his life could be something large and belong to the world.

But the world threw him upside down, the roadside bomb did, and when the truck he was riding in came to rest, all of the soldiers inside were thrown out of the hatches, and some of them were on fire. Everything comes from the side of the road over there, every form of death. Everyone dies in something exploded, and the photographs have no humans in them, only tendrils and wilted petals of iron.

Though it was hard to believe, and though they'd thought they'd learned about these things from Tim's father's war, the funeral took place in a divided town. The larger group that opposed the war were spurned by the many who supported it. The family wasn't that way, of course. They were kind, with the kindness of the stunned. They looked like sleepwalkers in a fog, struggling to reach out and shake people's hands like blind men.

There were arguments out at the edges of the gathering, at the peripheries. If people started debating something, they had the good manners to cross the street away from the mismatched brick and siding-fronted funeral home. But you could hear them. They sort of growled at one another, and the sound of it carried along in the wind. Maybe that is where Hadley got the idea of Mrs. Garner roaring, of a loud, bruised sound coming up out of someone's chest.

Hadley had to keep away from the arguing, milling people. She saw there were people on the roof, on a sort of balcony. She left the front step and came back inside. The coffin was silver, right in front of her, and she bent her face over the strange, scratched piece of glass or plastic that covered it, a structure separate from the lid.

His face was fine, with no wounds. Not even a mark. Life seemed long ago to have stopped its journey through his tensed muscles, lightening his limbs, streaming into his heart. His skin had turned very brown in the sun. The spaces around his eyes had narrowed so that, even with them shut, he looked as if he could have been Asian.

The more Hadley looked at him, the more she saw a completion in the new-colored, smooth skin of his cheeks and forehead, in the unimaginable worlds it had absorbed. Why do we feel we have to own the future along with everything else? Who says his purpose was to live into a future? Maybe his purpose was to be just what he had been: someone fighting with his comrades, for a cause he believed he served and that served him, and in which his short life had found its place and fruition. She had to believe he had taken with him the world he was meant to be given. She thought of Anchises, standing on the far bank in the Underworld, and saw Tim's casket glass as Lethe water, and saw him as happy and proud in his bed of flowers.

41.

Hadley is lying in bed with Jed. He kisses her, his mouth closing over hers, and she runs her tongue around his tongue and up across his teeth and along the soft ridge of gum that anchors them, and she is home. He was the first boy she ever met who really knew how to kiss. She thinks some have to be taught. Like dancing, it doesn't come naturally to some men. They are too forward looking to enjoy it, too anxious to get onward and downward. It was true when she was sixteen and it is just as true now.

They are lying on a thick-cushioned chaise on Jed's father's second story deck, and the Valley lights are stretched like tamped, kicked-apart coals through the muddy haze of the tule fog. Radio towers throb small lights and then go black. Planes drift down toward Burbank Airport, their beacons on and their gears going down.

She is in his mouth again. Sometimes they are like this for hours, not talking.

But now is when she notices something: the dents where his gums have softened, the places where the ephedra has washed away the periodontal tissue right where his teeth come out.

The rest of his mouth seems fine. This is the only place she can feel any give in the muscle. It is the stuff which, later on, you see in horrible color pictures in the magazine stories, before and after companion images, with the "after" being bright skin full of even brighter sores and abscesses: blackish, festering rat holes with flaking edges that show chemicals eating tissue and tissue eating itself.

No other drug does this. No other recreational chemical. Nothing people smoke or shoot or ingest. No kind of powder, liquid, spansule, syrette, plant, louvenee. Nothing. No thing.

This was the body going back to its vegetable state, the process of putrefaction that Dr. Adair, D.D.S., liked to relate when he tugged at her gums with his barbed aluminum retractors.

This is what is happening to Jed, what his body is beginning to undergo. When he pulls off of Hadley and lies there breathing, she thinks of the city as a giant reclining man in Dr. Williams' poem, stretched out along the Jersey Palisades with his back made of boulders and ancient granite ribs and his hair full of waterfalls, heavenly mists.

Sections of Paterson city's body rots, the neighborhoods peeling away in rust and flake, trees dying and sending sidewalks up like boils from swelling, bulging roots. The polis becomes unsalvageable and putrid, returning to brambles, thickets, devouring soils.

Jed is rotting like this, like the stone Leviathan. It is his doing, but after awhile that modest causation gets rolled up into natural pressures and flows, currents and countercurrents, the stiffening and then softening excrescences, the work of decrease. The earth is grabbing him back, grabbing back his clay and animate dust.

He is rotting, rotting. The thing that Hadley loves is rotting, breaking away into its raw materials. *I am dying, Egypt, dying.* He is leaving the flow, the flow leaving him, the water-giving streams slowing down to fallow, filling a fallow delta.

He breathes harder now when they make love. Under him, she sees the lights of the Valley off her right arm, like a fallen crystal bracelet. He breathes and breathes. The sweat on his shoulders dries. "We need to talk," he says.

42.

Jed tells Hadley that Darko has bowed out of all meth business and is working in larger stuff, smack and crack cocaine. Darko has put Jed in charge of all AF— alternate financing—for crank, which means all non-substance sales, all materials purchase and jacking, start-up costs, check washing, mail theft, and, and this is where his voice drops, *current projects*, by which he means the Clovis bank jobs.

When she tells him the new arrangement means he has more control, that the bank stuff can be canned, he is already shaking his head.

"I can't mess with anything that's already in place. Those skids were greased a long time ago."

"A long *time* ago? It's a bunch of Russians. They'll do it for somebody else, for *something* else, some other time."

He pulls himself up on the lounge until his back is at an angle, almost sitting up, and pulls the blanket up around his knees. The valley fog is thickening, the lights dimming.

"The fuse has been lit, Hadley. It's all ready to go."

"Funny way of running things, don't you think? Running things gets you *more* exposed? That being in control means you're *less* in control? You're the financer. You control the conditions. *You* say what goes forward and what doesn't."

"That's the sweetness and light version, Had. Some things get set, and the boss's goal—new boss, old boss—is to run them through."

"So let me get this right. You're more foregrounded now, but you can still stay as detached as the Hollywood job. And at the same time you can't call it all off. *That's* outside your power."

She waves her hand out at the Valley.

"Too good," she says, "still spells 'to be true.'"

"There's risks, Had. You know that. Like always. But we're as invisible as we were back over the ridge. The Russians don't know I've been promoted, which means the cops sure can't."

"The Russians are still talking to Darko? He's staying in for this?" She notices his eyes have gone blank again, filling with the window's light. Dust rises up around them in the shafts of it. It, the sunbeams, look almost liquid, clear as wine.

"Jed!" Hadley yells, but he won't turn his head.

She looks up and sees it, the inky sky, and then, as if in counterpoint to the basin below them, what people might actually live here for: a night of growing, cold clear stars.

When Jed looks back, Hadley sees what she expects: the Blanks, the Blankies, the Vacants, the Wasties. Is he lying or does he really not know? She figures now it's about six or seven on the lie meter— no way will they call Darko if something goes haywire, though maybe the key men, the ones Darko hooked up for the B. of A. job, would keep him on speed dial no matter what. After all, Darko's a Serb, Jed is a Valley rat. The Slavs take care of their own. The East is East, and the West can only guess at what it does.

There's something else now that makes Hadley think Jed knows he's in the soup, in the bull's-eye for the Clovis jobs, and that he's trying to bullshit her. It's the Loops, and it's a sure sign somebody is traveling at a pretty plastered altitude, and the truth function has a back seat to everything else. His words start to fly out in grandiose spasms, the kinds of things addled, homeless guys will erupt with when they are walking along and the world starts tilting away from them.

Jed will throw in phrases about ages and primordial forces. He tacks them onto offhand comments about the heat, the traffic, the way Darko ignores one of his men. Large reams of extra speech seep up from the simplest statements, spools of meanings and tones and colors, edgy, unworldly, unconnected to anything but a single word in the straightforward statement that has served as some kind of springboard into Jabberwock. He says the jobs he does are loaded with doom. He talks about new historical periods ushered in by sandstorms, or how the eyes of a sales clerk hold a soul he knew in other times and as some kind of other creature. In every mouthful there is something disassociated and horribly swollen. And he speaks it as if he's telling her the time, as if he's describing an errand he needs to take care of. Right now, lying here, he talks of the traffic below them, the common bumper-to-bumper crawling up the passes to Mammoth, as if it was a river of magnetism, a path of primordial messages. A fiery sign of something, a prophecy.

It's no different, Hadley understands, than what writers do, or what editors want writers to do. But it comes in the middle of normal talking. We're not set up for it. It's a change in the language game. She looks at him and waits for him to pause and laugh at what he's said. But then he says something just like it again.

Tonight, though, the drift of stars, the clearness of the sky has her determined to ignore this logorrhea, just this once, just this moment. She knows that she'll make her mind up soon enough about the Clovis job. Tonight is not to solve things, but to mold herself against him like the Western geography, like the little states on her maps: her Arizona folded into his Morales, her Oregon up against his Idaho, her strong spine of Colorado mountains nestled against his welcoming Utah, his big cold flat Nebraska.

Hadley is in love tonight, still, and likes being in love, even if not with the one long and true and final one to be loved. She worships love, or at least leans earnestly into its orbit like a weary, heavily-laden pilgrim. So there is no harm in ignoring all but his being her Pan tonight, her Pan and Cupid, her Christ, as Mr. Lowell said, of Love's religion.

43.

Back in the magazine office, night again, Hadley is curled up in the window space. The submissions pile is under her bent knees, and the editing pencils sit in a tall plastic purple cup that says "Kenyon" on it, white letters above a white shield.

One story really got her today. She thinks this writer really has the groceries, really has the stuff. This is a story with legs, on a whole other level than what she's been seeing. The narrator is a woman who lives somewhere in Arizona and keeps writing her parents that she is working with the developmentally disabled, the slow readers, so they will stay off her back. They are an old Eastern family and Mom and Dad are wondering when she'll return to Wellesley, back to summers as a counselor at Buck's Rock. All the acronyms she uses for the phony programs are plausible like "R.E.A.D." and "A.S.S.I.S.T." But none of them are true, and she realizes that her letters home are starting to get inconsistent with the acronyms and their phony program descriptions.

What the narrator is really doing is giving swim lessons to very old people in a landlocked city in the north, miles, maybe hundreds of miles, from any body of water. Almost nothing really happens in the story, and she tells the reader that right up front. But then she starts describing how she teaches these senior citizens techniques she actually had to teach when she was on her high school swim team back in Connecticut. One of the old ladies, named Kelda, said they were all obviously very lucky to have a swim coach living in town, and that it was sad there wasn't a lake or a pool or even a very large, rich person's bathroom with a significant bathtub where they could practice what she was teaching them. The narrator doesn't say much. She just nods at the old people's comments, their expressions of gratitude, and follows through with modest, usually hilarious, instruction keyed to each of their requests.

She teaches them how to breathe on a basic crawl stroke by putting big pans of water beside low cots. They dip their faces in and lift them out and turn them to one side to gulp in air, then put them back in the water and blow the air out. Two of the ladies are in their nineties and have never even tried to swim. They lived in Arizona all their lives and never even saw the Colorado River, no lakes, not even the lake where the London Bridge was rebuilt. They are thrilled to be learning everything, realizing it may be the last big life experience they have.

She teaches them all the strokes she knows. The Crawl is just as described, with the students dipping their faces and pumping their arms on each side of the cots, which must be thin enough to be stretchers left behind by some ambulance or medical transport vehicle. Their kicks can be vigorous, and the narrator assures the reader they are, because the cots are also too short for all of them. If their shins get bumped, she puts a towel or pillow down, though they protest this is too much, it's not necessary, they don't want her to go to such lengths of indulgence. Their gratitude is like their gratitude at being alive at their age. The amazing thing is that none of them are crotchety. None of them have any bitterness, and none of them give up on any part of the lessons.

None of them ever misses one, or comes late. She doesn't get paid for the lessons. The reader gets the feeling there is nothing else going on in the town at all, and that it really isn't a town so much as some kind of gas station with a motel-restaurant combination next door.

When it comes to the sidestroke there isn't any face dipping in the pans, the don't have to put their faces in the water at all. The butterfly is the most hilariously described. A guy named Jack Jack (yes, first and last name) flies across the floor throwing his winglike arms up feverishly, his belly smacking down, and his chin pushing the pan of water along the carpet from one end of the room to the other, never missing a dip-and-breathe. Sometimes the narrator is afraid of him dying and has him slow down. The bottom of his neck, right over the thyroid, gets flushed and folded with soggy pieces of carpeting and his own slobber. The harder he breathes, the happier he seems.

The narrator says things like, "If I can say this without being immodest, I was *instead* of the water." It's lines like that that make Hadley lose it, that make her want to look, if she has to, through a thousand stories for something that perfect. The pitch and tone are perfectly zany like that, colored with wonder but also mild irritation. The narrator describes barking out her instructions like a true competitive coach and blowing her whistle and having them spin around in unison when they hit their imaginary wall, and start swimming in the other direction. Then she has them *start diving*, one following the other, with each poised on a desktop, then timidly pushing off and belly-flopping onto a mattress (not a cot). Another thing she says: "It was still diving, it was still letting go of mammalian pride and giving in to gravity's hug." When one of the ladies suggests they make noises as they land, the narrator says it is a little too creative for her taste, but that she wants to be the kind of teacher who learns from her students.

Later, when she sees them in the parking lots of the completely non-existent stores and village establishments, the narrator asks them if they have been practicing their dives and strokes, and they say things like:"I'm working on it, Coach!"

The story peters out a little when it weaves back into messages she wants to leave her mean boyfriend, the who, along with her parents, drove her to these ends of the earth, to this moonscape of a state, "four hundred square miles of kitty litter." Hadley thinks the lines are perfect. They come with the spice of somebody doing stand-up, and when she finds the contributor's bio, she won't be surprised if she's also a performance artist or something like that.

All of their submissions are blind. Hadley settled on this method after hearing that one of the editors of the *Best American Short Stories* used it so he wouldn't be better disposed toward his friends, names he recognized, people who were big at the moment. So Hadley asked that people not put their name on until the last page, and then fold the page in fours, still keeping it stapled, so the reader has to take a minute to unfold it and can't be picking it apart while reading.

Hadley is blown away by the story. She's both still laughing and actually trembling a little at its quality, almost intimidated to have something this good make its way to her. She opens the four-squared last page.

The name is there, for some reason in the lower left corner, and with an email address underneath. It's Natasha. Natasha Varvouchka, the burned girl.

44.

Jed comes in the next day, right during Hadley's sustained high on the Natasha story, and tells her that the hour is nigh, the time has come round at last, hesitations have to be set aside and decisions made. The roads must roll. It is like Normandy, so much bigger than they are.

"Had, they gave me, Darko gave me, a second. Somebody to lead the whole group of Russians into their positions. If there is anyone being watched, it'll be them. Our convoy is just to spot, to give map back-up, the same as last time." He nods over to the urn the maps are in. "Can you start marking in the next few days? We want to get up there by this Thursday night. We have a one day window."

He pulls out his Djarums, and she motions that she wants one, and sees that he takes this as a sign of hopefulness. They light them and she pulls the lid from a jellybean jar over and turns it upside down for ashes. It is still day, blazing day. No reflections in the windows.

"Just do the markings with the algos we got in. Just put them in."

She takes a draw. She sighs and lets out the smoke.

"*Had*," he says. He rests his elbows on his knees, not taking his eyes off her.

After half a minute he tells her she doesn't even have to go if she doesn't want. He just needs the notations. He just needs the numbers that only she can do, crossed in. He just needs, just needs.

Hadley thinks of Natasha's image of the elderly swimmers, grateful, blurting out their enthusiasms, so misplaced and comical that they finally become perfectly placed, perfect little pieces of the crazy overall enterprise. The narrator was wondering if the butterfly swimmer, Jack Jack, was hitting his chest too hard on the floor with each stroke, and when she went up to him, he assured her that no, he'd lived three times her lifetime, and that he wouldn't do anything he knew would hurt himself or any of the others. And then *she*, the narrator, undergoes new waves of flattery, humility, blandishments, new surges of genuine admiration for her charges. Hadley wonders if one of the messages of the story is that kindnesses, simple acts of grace and love, are only found in futile and absurd enterprises, and that doing something genuinely constructive needs at least one or two ends-means people—agendized, mercenary, possibly sadistic.

Jed seems to think he is asking so little of her, and maybe he is. Could she really stay back, or would it be one of those situations where he came in at the end, as the engines were warming up, and scooped her away with one of his *must must* entreaties?

And the Second. Who was the Second? Who *was* he really? How powerful? Did he have a trail of people with him? If they were really decoys for Jed and Hadley, then why not have them do actual tasks, real work on the job? Two whole crews weren't necessary for a cow town knockover. And the job would have to yield a lot to pay two crews. New people were less people you could be certain of, less people you could trust: the longer the chain, the weaker the link sort of thing.

"Had," he says. "the chance of anything going bad here is, like, *nothing*. This isn't the LAPD the crew is up against. It's Barney Fife."

She laughs. "With his one bullet?"

"Maybe two, maybe ten. But it's *Clovis*." He smiles and picks a seed from his teeth.

"The Second. Who is he? Have you met him?"

"Totally. He's straight as a Moscow yardstick. Name's Sergei. Right off the boat, but speaks English like a pro."

"Most of them do."

"Most smart ones. Most like this. He was—"

"Wait, let me guess, a safecracker, I mean an *engineer....*"

"Over there, right. He was."

Voices outside in the hallway are asking each other where the magazine is. Hadley looks at Jed and puts her finger over her lips. Then she thinks it may be Natasha. Or another Natasha.

"Sergei was running concerts for awhile in the Baltic countries. You know, Sting, the Stones, the Dead. The Dead were huge there. They sponsored the Latvian basketball team in the Olympics. The jerseys were tie-dye, I shit you not."

He lifts another Djarum out of the pack and lights the new one with the old. This is something Hadley has never seen him do, seen anyone do, with a perfumed cigarette.

"He was in with some of the American roadies. He helped set up the old sound system, the big Uroburos thing—the wall of sound— they had during the early seventies. He's a handsome guy. He started going out with one of the band member's wives. He got her pregnant."

Jed's voice lifts, takes on a tiny lilt, and Hadley can see that a Loop is coming. It is like one of the balloon men on the Promenade putting the lip of rubber over the helium nozzle, watching the long flaccid thing start to rise and bob to stiffen out.

"Yeah, I mean, I can't even tell you which guy in the band it was. But her husband was all ready to have it and she wanted an abortion, and he said no. So she had Sergei's baby, who is the third kid of this guy, grown up. I think he's a filmmaker now."

Then the next parts of the story come, and Sergei had traveled on with the Dead and with other bands, and was running Alembic, the instrument company Garcia founded in the early Seventies. Then he was with the band in Riga when they got nailed for pot, and was working at the very highest levels of the KGB and *militsa* to get them all out on bond so they could play a gig the same night. Then he ended up seducing another player's wife. Then *they* had that kid. So the story has this guy populating an entire generation of the group, sort of like Marianne Faithful was with each of the Stones, sleeping with each of the new band members, like she was the welcome wagon or something.

But then Jed has Sergei piloting their plane, or their helicopter, or something. He has him producing all their shows. Sergei has a sixth sense about appropriate venues, sound quality of certain halls, what the weather will do for this or that stadium show. The guy is really like a shadow group member, taking them to post-Soviet palaces

   RICHARD WIRICK

and resorts, engineering all the unpredictable stages of that kind of road work. Jed says he was a child prodigy and got into engineering school at eleven or twelve, then worked on Soviet nuclear projects, the heavy water experiments at Akademgorsk. He was a particle theorist who was also a hippie that they watched like a hawk and covered with counter intelligence, but he was able to wear his hair and clothes like he wanted, they let him keep his hangdog rocker look.

Then Jed is looping farther and farther outward, with stories of the guy hiding people inside of mountains during undecipherable insurgencies that fit no historical context. He has him mixing drugs and running microfilm across borders, helping to set up orphanages and reconstructing the destroyed water treatment plants of Sarajevo. In the middle of it all Jed will say something like, "He's quieter than you think," or "You'll find him a perfect gentleman." But then he'll go right back to the superhuman, with semi crashes narrowly averted by the man's clairvoyant driving and gigs (yes, he stayed with the band) salvaged from stalled visas and singers' laryngitis and extended methadone hangovers. Sergei is like Prospero, like a radiant Sun, the planets spinning around him, brightening or darkening with his nods and offhand pointing fingers. He knows all heads of state in those regions, or, more importantly, knows the heads of the secret police. The entire military-repressive apparatus is at his disposal, along with, apparently, the weather, the moods of audiences, the color of the leaves in forests they pass on the Autobahn.

Jed goes out and back, out and back. He ties Sergei into everything, all that's past, passing, or to come. Meanwhile the guy tunes everybody's guitars and repairs organ consoles and synthesizers.

A pair of feet stop in front of the door. A small pile of papers, somebody's story, slides in.

45.

Hadley's father is sitting in his studio, asleep in his chair. In front of him is a blueprint of a great, arched wing of an aircraft that will never be built. The Republicans have come back to Congress and such projects are again going into hiatus. The webbed, perfectly-notched half-moon on the paper might as well be a bridge span, something out of Calatrava. It would have just as much of a chance of flying.

When Hadley opens the door and wakens him, he starts. He's covered himself with his cardigan. When the lights come up, his eyes are red. He's still thinking of Timmy, who'd been one of his Boy Scouts in the Kern County troop he led for awhile in the eighties.

She wraps her arms around him from behind.

"It's why I went to Canada," he says. "Right when his Dad was in Tran Nang."

"And I'm grateful that you did. I, for one, am grateful."

He gathers his markers and puts them in their plastic boxes. When each box is full he puts it into its rack.

"*Quick eyes gone under the earth's lid,*" he says. "He was gone that quick. The *meaning* in that line."

Hadley searches for it.

"Hugh Selwyn Mauberly," she says.

Her father smiles. "And it was about an artist, it was about Gaudier-Brzeska."

"Twenty-five years old."

"Twenty-seven. Timmy," he says, and his eyes well up.

"I feel guilty I didn't try to stop him."

The wing of the plane has black, spidery girders, with the checkering inside the structure as clear and detailed as an architect's drawing. It looks capable of *being* a building, of providing shelter.

"Like I was clearing him out, waiting for him to go."

"Don't think about that, honey. He wanted to go as sure as you wanted the slot. People know what they're doing. People choose."

"He chose to be outside phalanx cover? He didn't have a vest. You can't choose *not* to have what they don't have for you."

"There was an article in the *Times* today on equipment shortages."

"Yeah," he says, "I read that."

"Did you like him back then? As a Scout? Was he a nice kid?"

"He was full of it, the routine. He was born to it."

"I thought his Dad was pretty even-keeled about it all. I mean, being in Nam."

"Born to it," he repeats.

"But his Dad didn't stay in. He wasn't a lifer."

Hadley's father grabs her hands on his shoulders, looks up at her.

"Didn't have to be. All it takes is a word or two. A look. That's how a kid takes signals. Impressions. Like prints in wet clay."

"But he was *hip*, Daddy. He wasn't a stiff. He was the one who snapped up the craziest stuff. Pushed for the Gonzo."

"There's all kinds of stuff in the same person. The mix is never clear, just that there's a mix. That's what's clear. Look at that Haanson guy they caught selling secrets to the Russians. *Opus Dei*. Five kids. *Eagle Scout*. But he got people killed, and all for money. And screwed anything that walked."

"But it was a good mix in Tim. Good with good. It's just the military thing was. . .skewered, mysterious. Out of left field."

"Not out of left field. Out of the cradle. Out of the first moments, the first hours and days."

"God, the girders there. It's like it's alive. An eagle's wing."

He points to the angle at the apex of the span. "Kind of the idea."

Hadley kisses the top of his head and turns to go.

"Honey."

"Yes, Daddy."

"Keep yourself safe. Like Ginsberg said, 'Be kind to yourself/It is only one/ And perishable of many on the planet.'"

"I am. I will."

But she never knows what he knows about her, and when she sees him looking at her hands now, unsteady, still slightly trembling and with scratch marks on the bottoms of the palms, she sees him wondering.

"I am," she says again, reaching for the door. "I will."

46.

While Hadley is watching Jed's crew prep for the trip, the leaves begin to fall. Yes, leaves; it's not all palms and yuccas here. In fact, the high desert has a wintry flora, and when Fall comes they can almost get the full New England: good, long-lasting patches of yellow and crimson on the ground. Long-lasting because nobody rakes them.

From her father's porch, Hadley can make out Darko's former girls, the check washing chicks, the new Triangle Garment workers, one by one, bringing stuff out of his house and into the two cars and the trailer parked, still unattached, behind the El Camino. Most of what they're hauling is just backpacks and piles of folded clothes. But they're also bringing wash pans and large manila envelopes that must have checks in them.

A plastic tarp lays beside the Camino bed, rippling and sparkling in the wind. It has stretch ropes tipped with small hooks that aren't heavy enough to keep it from dragging, so the thing lifts in the gusts and the ropes spin and wag like little tendrils. It all looks, from this high up, like a swollen amoeba or fine-haired sea urchin.

Jed shows up in the doorway with a clipboard, looking like a contractor. He's even wearing khaki pants.

One of the girls stands in the doorway talking to him, putting her hands on her hips and cocking her head, bending over in mock laughter at things he says. Sometimes he acts like he's chasing her away, swinging the clipboard at her butt as she dodges him. She coyly scampers back, with her head down.

Everyone else is coming and going with the packing, ignoring them, ignoring whatever he's occasionally telling them.

Even from this distance Hadley can tell the girl is pretty. She has blonde short-cropped hair that lifts over her peasant blouse in the breeze.

So many of this crew of girls are blonde. It's as if a family of Swedish daughters came down from Solvang, helping the druggies with their day labor.

Hadley remembers the movie "The Time Machine," how her sixth grade teacher had extolled it and how she wasn't disappointed. When Rod Taylor journeys forward in time and encounters the slave race of Eloi, all of them look like this—Nordic and limber, gentle and obedient, Grecian in their calm and blind, almost, to the feelings of others, which they seem as incapable of digesting as an Asperger's patient.

Parking the cars, these girls look no different than Weena, the Eloi love of Taylor, played by Yvette Mimieux before she went on to become the Chapstick queen. Hadley remembers how Taylor tries to awaken a sense of responsibility in her after she stands by and watches a friend drown, how he tries to give her an awareness of past and future, the value of history and historical knowledge. Jed reminds Hadley of Taylor now, trying to wrangle a meandering herd into some kind of effective group.

And the Morlocks, the people who've subjugated the Eloi: these are Darko's men, the Russians and the Russians' helpers, the Romanians in their fearsome battle dress. They live under the ground, in holes that look like wells but are really smokestacks, seeping and exhaling ether.

In the doorway, the blonde girl looks to be taunting Jed. Their faces move close together but do not touch.

A wave of the jones goes through Hadley as she waits, watching. Or something sicker, deeper than the jones, something that she could never have dreamed of or expected.

47.

There are kite flyers and moto-crossers down in the scrub valley. Hadley's father's balcony is nice this way, with its long views, the green lawn going down the chasm into brown. Hadley's hands on the balcony railing make her think of Jed: her hard, sweet thing. If staying with him or going was the same, to the extent she could always come back, they why not just go? And she thinks, *because he chose me.* Of everyone here, it was me that he came for.

Last night in her room, she saw her reflection, and wanted to talk to herself like she did those nights she was snorting and flying. But she saw how stringy her hair was. She saw the hollows under her eyes, the same blue bags her family has had for generations. Jed had looked past it all, looked past what was breaking down: her crooked eyes, the way her nose crinks slightly left. His love was certain, a certain thing, showing the value of something over nothing. It was, as the poet says, what someone talked about when they talked about love. Or what they talked about when they talked about faith: something waiting there, quietly, for you. That you climbed up onto and held through the tilt and wobble.

But Jed is shifting out of certainty, and it seems all Hadley knows now is what she can build on each day: putting the sentence down and turning it around, slicing off adverbs and adjectives, reading it to someone and waiting for the recognition in their face.

Stringing the words together, getting them out—that was the uncertain, the unsure, the wait for the listener's recognitions. Tim had told her the story of the young poet and Berryman. "How can you know?" the young man asked, "that what you write will ever last? How can you ever, ever be certain?" And Berryman said: "You can't. You can never be certain. If you want to be certain, then don't do the difficult thing. Don't write."

Some people see crosses and visions in clouds. Jennifer Jones, in the movie *Bernadette*, saw the Virgin, hanging like a pretty vampire in the air. The thing Hadley wants to be certain, that kite? Up there darting and whirling and dipping? She *knows* it can crash, get tangled up in itself, that it might not *even be there*. Might be dust on her eyeball, a piece of confetti. Really, there is only tension in its line, rattling in the wind and pulling at her hands. That restlessness, tugging her, has to be it. That is her faith.

The whole hillside of grass changes direction, like hair flopping over. Cold, wet, rapid drafts fill her nose, smelling of sod. She knows, just as she smells it, that she doesn't need Jed. She doesn't *need* him, doesn't have to have him. But she can still want him, she can still love him. Though the heart, she knows, never fits its wanting.

There are ATVs. little off-road devices, moving up the graveled mountainside beyond the pastures. They are ugly little things, hideous like bugs, with the drivers also hideous in their goggles and helmets. The one she sees now sends up a sweet, coloring cloud, symmetrical as waves on each side of its tires. It is ugly, but moving as sure as an angel. It is battered, but cheerful. It sputters, moves up.

48.

Hadley is marking the maps in a room at the back of the Palmdale library. First she xeroxed them, taped the separate pages together, put a stiffer backing on the dupe, and now she's sat down with a chai from Caribou and her purple cup of markers and compasses and miniature T-squares. She's taking up two tables and praying that the usual no one who comes here stays usual, stays no one.

She's doing enhances to the old versions. She hasn't worked with them in a while, so the colors seem off, the shine on the plastic bothers her. The markers don't even feel right in her hand.

They're not the right density. The plastic *is* thicker and she has to press harder than she ever has. Or is she imagining this, backwashed with the zaps and still sad about Tim and nervous, nervous about Clovis.

She takes deep breaths. The chai calms her. Caribou's branding is impressive. Their valley is too grubby for Starbucks, so it was the stag that had to migrate here.

She puts four rows of numbers into the red asterisks that signal gravel deposits. She puts another four rows under the puffs of orchard blue, hillocks of coke and swag, and the last four (it takes an hour) in tree-specks swiped across knolls of yellow and rusty-orange sand.

There is a group of tiny figures that look like stick men. The map key says they are limestone shills, lips of other compounds that settled into this kind of rock over a period of a quarter million, a half million years. This is where, according to the formula, she is supposed to put the last number series, a group three times the length of the usual four.

The blonde girl in the doorway yesterday with Jed. Hadley had seen her before. She was the one Darko had thrown the shed panel open for on their first drive downtown, had kissed in the daylight, and then had brought out to his truck.

She puts the numbers in now, sideways against the small human figures, thin as crosses, like she told Darko's guy she would. Each numeral is straight, with an elegant long back. A four, a one, many, many nines. They fit right under each little man's neck, clean and quick as a slicing blade.

49.

Hadley can't find Jed at the send-off party. One of the girls organized it to celebrate what they all think is really just another relocation of a lab and washing room. Only the few who know about the Clovis job realize what is really being celebrated. But it is an old-time, big-time blast, a mosh pulsation, big and loud and heavy with bass thumps.

Most everybody seems to have gotten here high. But in the first room off the front, the lines are being laid out, people bend down over cardboard boxes, and beyond, in the hallways, smoke rises up and hangs in long, solid, cottony blocks just under the ceiling. The smell of everything, even the furniture, is of mildew and match smoke and camphor.

The crowd seems a lot younger than at most crank parties. Small, thin-waisted girls with no breasts and baby-fat faces take long draws on cigarettes and look exceedingly uncomfortable, smelling and registering forbidden space. Their chopped, spiked hair is brightly cellophaned: orange, pool water blue, magenta, pulsing and swaying like casino neon.

It's hard for Hadley to tell anyone's age anymore, especially people younger than her. The three *devochka* she watches now could be eight, they could be fifteen. The obligatory bra straps are exposed and their broad black Mexican belts are covered with menacing rivets. All childhood seems to be sexed up now, or there just *is* no childhood.

One of them stamps on her cigarette and wanders over to a strung-out boy tapping drum beats on his knees. She flops down on his lap and reaches around to his back pocket for something, cigarettes, a handkerchief. He's indifferent. She could be a tree branch fallen on him, a thrown coat or a roll of towels.

But she turns around and tips his chin up and kisses him bang on the lips, then up the bridge of his nose and once on each eye, his forehead, his hair. Her hands stay closed and her knuckles run along his scalp like she's giving him a Dutch rub. She hops off and pulls him into the hall, slamming him against the smeared sheetrock until he comes alive, pressing his thigh against her crotch and rolling his head with the kiss. The blue smoke lays over them, drifting backward over their backward walking like a poison barge.

The boys the other boy was with are looking at Hadley as she watches. One of them nods at her and she turns away.

She walks to the back porch to look for Jed. Across the lawn, under two or three low floodlights, the full Boschian esplanade is assembled. Speakers inside of rocks are blasting ancient nineties material: Foo Fighters, Sonic Youth, System of a Down. Dancers fasten their bodies like colors molding in pools, peeling off shirts, knee-length basketball trunks, kicking shoes off into the moistening lawn. Glass salad bowls of pills lie on long cafeteria tables, bongs, crack pipes, burning incense cones. The people dancing don't look at each other at all. They don't feel the nacho chips and plastic wine glasses their bare feet stomp on. They all clap, but at different times.

More kids stand back by the fences, passing around pipes and plates of food. Some are down on the ground on top of each other. Some are passed out. Dogs wander through the grass, licking the dropped plates.

Hadley keeps looking for Jed. She can't find him anywhere.

A girl with short blonde hair wanders outside the far right fence corners, the ember of her cigarette lighting her face as she lifts it. It could be the one who kissed Jed or it could be any of the others Hadley saw yesterday. And besides that, she could be imagining all that transpired in that doorway. She could be wrong. But there's a spark of certainty here this time, a glimmer, a flash from some core of deep wanting.

The blonde girl wanders back and forth, her head held high but twitching freakishly as she lights one cigarette after another. She's looking for someone the same as Hadley is, the same wild horse running away over the hills.

　　　　　　　RICHARD WIRICK

50.

It's Leaving Day. It's Exodus. When Hadley pulls into Jed's and puts the Escort behind the cement block dumpster corral, the maps in the back seat tumble forward and two long tubes hit her in the back of her head. Her backpack is in the back, too, stuffed with a couple of outfits and her rubber-banded together books, and the only thing in the trunk is water—four boxes of two-litre Sparkletts. She would have packed real food, but the few girls who were going with them haven't seen anything but take-out since birth, and will be eating it throughout this trip and for all eternity.

When she comes around front holding the maps, she sees Jed standing, looking at the two cars and the trailer attached to the El Camino. She stands beside him, smelling his wet, shampooed hair and the Djarum smoke that never leaves his clothes. He asks her what she thinks. She tells him it's like a wagon train, and it's his ass that's going to have to keep them from the Indians.

"You got water in the trunk?"

She nods and hands him the keys.

The bed of the El Camino has the tarp packed down hard around it, tucked in, the elastic ropes hooked with military precision. A smaller piece of the same tarp lies over the trailer hooked onto the back, with its corners pulled back for the water and Hadley's maps. There is a three or four foot space in the back of the El Camino bed, enough for a couple of people to sit in facing backwards, like those fancy leather Volvo rumble benches, and which make Hadley wonder what they are doing with a trailer anyway. When she goes over to put the maps in, she smells the camp stove propane, and sees the olive drab canisters of it piled beside grills and other pieces of two or three Colemans. There are lanterns, boxes of blue tip matches and wood for campfires. A wet line runs around the seam of one of the small tankards, and Hadley makes sure nobody comes near it, especially nobody who is smoking.

The maps feel like paintings to her, like she is a high-priced transporter of centuries-old canvases covered with reams of indemnity agreements and closed-circuit television security. She puts the backpack down and lifts out a stained T-shirt she planned to throw out after wearing it one last time. She puts the T-shirt down on the trailer bed and lifts some of it up toward the tanks, folding it double where it lies against the leaking one. She takes the four maps and runs a six foot plotch of binder twine around them, puts them in a big throwaway plastic ski bag for checked luggage ("Delta Airlines") she finds covering the already padded lanterns, and lays them in gently as she would a baby, like Moses's mother pecking him on the forehead and sliding him into the bulrushes. She separates the tops so the four rolls support each other, reinforcing their own angles of repose like willow branches in an urn.

Jed comes back with two of the boxes of water and again makes his case for putting the maps inside one of the cars, they're that important, they're not just staples and ballast. But for some reason Hadley finds herself telling him no, that the water should go in the cabs because they'll need it most of all, sooner than they think, with this Hell Itself weather revving up to intolerable temperatures before most people are even out of bed. When Jed opens his mouth, Hadley takes the two boxes from him, tells him to get the other two, and heads toward the Mustang.

Pam and Susan, two girls Hadley met at the party last night, will ride with Jed. Hadley will go in the El Camino with two other girls she has yet to meet and with the driver, Detlef, one of Darko's former people, who is actually less scary than his colleagues, but still scary, a sort of Sinister Lite. She has had to handle him on some of the flower district trips. She always liked him because he *didn't* have a gun. He is supposed to be, like Neal Cassady, the Great Driver, the one who will keep the El Camino steady in the mountain foothills.

The two other girls come out and introduce themselves. One is Dakota, looking underage and over eye-shadowed and very bare-midriff, the long swath of skin running from pubis to breast bottoms almost the product of a soft porn draftsman, as though the whole length of her waist and belly and lower chest are some kind of flesh-colored creature of its own, elongated, stretched by a rack, *sinewy*. Her companion, the one who carries her cigarettes, is Ondaatja, a Sri Lankan girl who Hadley thinks has a day job at one of the Payday Advances on Myrtle Avenue. According to Jed, she's also a check washer, one of the Triangle Fire children, but seems determined to never say anything. She wouldn't scream if she was jumping off a sky-scraper.

For a minute or two before they climb in they all stand around, unintentionally, in a circle. When they notice, Pam giggles a little, says they should say a prayer, sing *Kumbaya*. Hadley shrugs. Jed is sucking the last, sweet blast of smoke from his Indonesian tobacco. The sun is up at full eight o'clock on the horizon now, making the hills of rocks around them sparkle, drying the dew off the Agave spears.

If a photographer were to shoot them from a hundred feet off, they would look no different than a bunch of Gypsies, a Roma cara-van getting ready for its next involuntary town-clearing. They are all young but, in their bent-over, pre-fatigued assemblage, they look like mule drivers and skinners, storytellers, village explainers, tinsmiths, horse thieves, cobblers and musicians. They are like the Romany who, when the Slovak fascists fabricated musical license requirements for them, buried their harps in the forest. Their poet wrote a ballad about the harps listening to the grass grow, listening to the empty sound of time's drum. The down vests they'll soon take off look velvet in the sunlight, and the cheap shoes they wear are like Roma slippers woven of hair, their toes curled up, their seams crooked and flashing bright like the streams in the black, far rocks.

And then they get in. Hadley is the last. A bead of sweat runs down her temple and, like a raindrop, drops on the canvas of her jacket.

* * *

As soon as they rise up into hills, Hadley can see the real, outward face of the earth her maps are the ancient and approximate voices of: woodlot sands and hills of pickle patches and field grass and hedges sloping down in natural emerald bowls. They go northwest toward Kern County, and in the far distance the Sierras watch them, mock those in the lowlands like giants watching mice from the corners of their eyes. The sun climbs, burning off the surface of the car's hood in waves along the bottom of the windshield. Hadley looks over at Detlef, but he will have none of her. He is a yeoman aspiring to be a journeyman. He will have no truck, so to speak, with the help.

The towns they see from the road are the same as their own. There are always the few long streets of boarded up stores and sundry shops, the one old abandoned theater that animals wander in and out of and that kids eventually burn down. The only signs of life at eleven of a Fall morning are the growing lines of people waiting to apply for unemployment at the EEOC offices. Surrounding all of this, like the rim of a butterfly net around the old town, the town proper, are the antiseptic clamps of freeway entrances and exits, and the mighty, white-lined miles of sleeping, new-laid stone. Farther up in the hills the hovels of neighborhoods wither like dying ivy. Water tanks whose legs have broken sink into the ground. The corral fences are broken but the livestock stay, nibbling the choppy trails of grass. Where would they go? As far as the eye can see there is no green.

In the farthest neighborhoods and unpaved crossroads, where there is only a shed or a trailer or two, or a car that people are living in, there are almost always dogs. Dogs are eaten in Siberia, especially, for some reason, pregnant dogs, and there is a wariness in these animals that is not seen in the smooth-brushed canines of Brentwood. These dogs sleep in deep piles of dust, their chains slack and their shit piles hardening into little hills around them. Their masters bring out motor oil cans of water and they bolt forward, their chains tightening like a hanged man's rope in free fall.

The ramshackle backs of the buildings and houses of towns that they pass look like the grainy footage of people waving at funeral trains of the famous dead: Lincoln and FDR and Bobby Kennedy, people standing away at the point of perfect focus, but stiff and bewildered with grief.

Try to imagine what it must be like for a passing *car* to be an event enough to look out on, to contemplate, to take away from the stiltedness of what surrounds. If they are not looking at the car, it is the sun to which they lift their faces. It must be even more of an oven for them, Hadley thinks, magnified by the huge blue sky.

She thinks of another Roma line. It is a song about the sun. *It is an angry, angry star,* the chorus goes, *It whispers only of your death.*

51.

The cars make their dogleg up 128 toward Fresno, and they are out of the brown at last now, heading into the peripheries of the Cleveland Forest. People who can't afford to live in the City, and can't even make it in the Valley—teachers, secretaries, service workers—live out in these Southern Kern Valley bedroom towns, driving as much as an hour and a half each way to places like Santa Monica.

And it's not a bad place to be. It's an Arden Forest compared to the miles and miles of sandbox sand that makes up the Antelope Valley. There are basins of Douglas Fir and juniper, and spruce so green and vast it burns the eyes. Down under the water line are deciduous trees that undulate from brown to yellow to russet and copper, all of them topped with a cobwebby silver of frost.

This is timber country, and when the clouds clear and the moon is bright, cross-cuts appear out of the high blue gloom, and toylike trucks descend white roads bent down with loads of tight-strapped logs. These are Cathedral Pines, churches of ten thousand steeples, with every watcher, including Hadley, appearing gratified to breathe and sigh and utter the note of the wonderstruck: Amens of great timbers, amens of great timbers.

To get some of this breath in her, she rolls the windows down, and Detlef has pulled up parallel with Jed, who is staring straight ahead, refusing to acknowledge them. He sucks on his Djarum, wipes the inside of his windshield with a Kleenex. How perfect. Here they are again, side by side on parallel paths, neither of them meeting or expecting to meet, anchored on their separate rails in the train station and only able to wave, not able to cross over into the other's cabin as the machines depart in their separate directions.

But Hadley takes her breaths anyway. It's been a long time since she's breathed like this. She takes in a gulp of air big enough to nearly choke herself, then lets it out slowly: Detlef looks at her weirdly, as if she's doing yoga. Then Hadley notices something.

What's making her breathe like this, slow and even, is that she can. Because she can't even feel a trace of the zaps anymore. All the weary sparking and saturation in the brainpan, all the slow, creepy voltage that climbed the walls and crossed the ceiling of her cranial vault these last few months—it's all gone. Vanished.

She looks down at her hands. They aren't trembling anymore. She has no need to still them. The bottoms of her palms aren't itching.

She is clean, washed empty of the stuff, at least for now. If she could open up the car's sunroof, if it had a sunroof, and emerge waist high into the mountain wind, the blue of the air would show through her like a window. There'd be outlines of her shoulders and chest and arms, and inside them only air, only azure, only pool water blue.

Her body is doing a lot of deciding now, like the body often decides. Thoughts can be the slowest kind of horse, the big ones they call dobbins, or the slow uneven road the horse gets lost on, pacing out its continuous circles.

But the body pulls. The body is the bridle. It can go one way; it can go the other. But it goes, its fearful hormones push.

Jed finally looks over at them, signals them all to pull over. And that's when Hadley decides, or something decides, that she wants to ride back in the truck bed.

52.

There, in the back, the tarp rattles loud, *really* rattles, loud as gunfire, its bright edges flying around her head. Her knees are right in her face there's so little room. It's bumpy, scary the way the whole thing swerves, and she has one hand on the tailgate and one on the tree branch she found at the rest stop, thinking she'd try carving it down into a walking stick.

These towns in the Kern forests are dead, especially dead in the slow times around the noon hour. No cars move anywhere and nobody walks the streets. The great carpet of trees lets no one in, not even the sun, and nothing emerges, not a dog or a pair of human legs or a bird.

Hadley looks down at the trailer hitch Jed had complained about, calling it cheap, calling it "nigger-rigged." It is really just a pin put through the common hole of the bulb of the trailer tongue and the primitive, twenty-dollar boat hitch is soldered so badly that big drip marks stick up like bubbles of tar. It also rattles, groans in high bat squeals with the trailer's weight.

It's a high wire she's out here on, *that's* the feeling, an endless, endless wire whipped by this wind and without a net or a balance bar, with only the fear-strength, only the never-sure, only the *you're never sure, if you have to be sure, don't do it.* Don't do it. Don't marry him. Don't write. Don't take the money and make the movie.

The body decides. The body decides or does not decide. The bridle pulls.

The trailer pin rattles. Its round, high fired handle end jingles.

Hadley gets up and lodges her knees against the bed, and then she leans out and wraps her fingers around the pin and pulls it up.

The trailer seems to stand still for a second in its unconnectedness, but then gets gulped away in the air, and in just a second or two it is twenty, forty, a hundred feet behind them, catapulting straight back into the empty lane before it swerves in a gust and begins to roll down the dusty mountainside. It spins maybe five, maybe six times before the orange explosion comes and the black smoke starts blowing sideways into the high scrub grasses.

53.

The trailer burned itself out at the bottom of the mountain. Hadley imagined the void that was left after the smoke rolled away. When Detlef saw that it had come loose, he just, out of instinct, gunned it. Jed said it was the Russian desire to get out of Dodge when something transpires that may get the attention of the watchers, the coppers, the ever-circling buzzards.

Of course, Hadley couldn't see the look on his face from where she was sitting. She couldn't see Jed's face either, or anybody's. They all just kept going. She leaned her head back onto the tarp and closed her eyes.

There was really nothing to report, because it wasn't an accident, the trailer not having hit anything. At least that's the way they saw it. So, after about twenty minutes, they pulled off, came back the frontage road until they found an entrance to an old state route, and took that back all the way into town. They didn't see any traces of the fire.

They gathered back at Jed's. People came back tired, hangdog-looking, but no one was really angry. No one had seen Hadley do it. No one had any suspicions. There could have been anything in that trailer—jewels, a human being, a couple of million dollars (and, in a way, there was, indirectly and in Jed's mind, with what her maps could have gotten them).

After she pulled the hitch pin, Hadley sat there like a soldier with a grenade. Then she'd let the pin go too, listening to it clank as it bounced off into the gravel. Back inside the house everything that Jed said was static, white noise. His face, and the faces of the others, had already begun to fade, to gel, to merge into one another. They were more like shapes of faces than actual likenesses, the kind of interchangeable globs seen in cloud formations and, if looked for very closely and if the light is right, in the bark of trees.

Jed said another trailer could be put together in a day or two, but it would have to be fast. They could have Hadley mark a second set of maps, but she would have to start on that sooner than fast, like that night. Like all night. This was the reason, he said, he'd wanted the maps in one of the cabs.

After about five minutes of map talk Jed sees Hadley looking at the door. Then he sees her stand up and he says her name. She is looking at the door as if it contains a window, as if she can see out of it with perfect clarity. And now she is moving toward some detail she's selected in the exterior landscape. Jed says her name again. Somebody coughs and she puts her hands in her jacket pockets.

As she keeps walking, she knows she is there, surrounded by those people, in that place, in that house, in that particular room. But she doesn't feel she is inside of anything. She doesn't feel, as she turns the doorknob, that anything can ever contain her again.

54.

There's a good crop of stories this week. They have some metafictional hi-jinks where the narrative is carried by a mathematical formula that speaks to another mathematical formula and a series of radar blips that have more character than a lot of, well, traditional characters. There's a story narrated by some kind of animal, a Patricia Highsmith kind of thing, where you know the animal's torturers are in for it but you can't stop turning the pages because you want to see exactly how. There's a traditional horror yarn involving a shotgun accident with a child, her faint rope-skipping jingles and the thud of the falling weapon echoing through the haunted barn like the Valley's familiar thunder.

The essays are good, too. They're getting a lot of stuff on the South Pacific, with Bikini atoll fallout causing serious turtle mutations and discolorations of the coral walls, divers coming down with skin irritations and hallucinations hundreds of miles off. One essay is written in short, separated paragraphs formatted like aphorisms, and deals with Darfur and the seeming futility of relief work. There's another one that argues against marriage as the primary organizational system for the life of an adult, even with children. There is one on Wahhabism and its effect on the inheritance of livestock and oases. One, that Hadley hasn't opened yet, is about "the scourge of Crystal Meth" in blue-collar, rural areas of the U.S. and Canada.

She followed her exit from Jed's place with a note to him. The note wasn't abrupt or unkind, but it didn't apologize for her decision, which was that she could never be with him in any way other than as a friend, and only after he cleaned up. She is afraid of being anywhere near him now. In fact, she has thought of getting a pistol from one of the Russians. When they pass each other in traffic, she sees him looking at her, and she stares straight ahead.

They say nothing is so hateful as the past one has left. Now that she's feeling good again, with her clear-as-a-windowpane blood, Hadley doesn't do any hating that she can consciously catch herself at. She knows, as Confucius said, that it makes her smaller. Besides, how can she hate what she actually *was*? The cells were different then but the brain and essential fluids were the same. Sometimes she wishes she had the whole wasted swath of time back. But she doesn't dislike what she was, or even what she did in those days. Regret grinds down the will, becomes its own strange form of self-consumption. It makes a person small, small as a neuron or a granule of dirt. Sometimes she looks out the window at the acres of blowing dust and imagines each tiny cloud as a host of the fallen, of people who petrified themselves with looking backward. And it makes sense that that's what they are now, something the wind carries away.

Natasha is Hadley's assistant editor now. They are dedicating the next issue to Tim. They're going to Hellenize this place, make it the next Marfa, Texas. Natasha's skin grafts are taking amazingly well. Hadley drives her up to UCSF for them every three weeks, and on the way back they raid the bookstores of Palo Alto and Berkeley and the Haight. Sometimes they sit up in the office's window seat at night.

With the two of them sitting there now, and with the good work they're doing, and even though it might be the worst kind of blind, blind, *uncertain* groping, Hadley knows there is no longer any duplication of herself, no splitting off into a Hadley this and a Hadley that. There's just the one rock solid flesh and blood of her, and the other a reflection, which is only a reflection. And both of them, or all four of them counting Natasha, are quickly scribbling, scribbling.

Richard Wirick is co-founder and editor of the journal *Transformation*. His work has appeared in *Playboy, Quarterly West, LA Weekly* and elsewhere. His earlier books include *One Hundred Siberian Postcards*, literary vignettes of his journey to Siberia to adopt a baby girl with his wife, and a book of interconnected stories, *Kicking In*. He practices law in Los Angeles, where he lives with his family.